THE SECRET OF THE
MINSTREL'S GUITAR

The Dana girls take time off from Starhurst School to accompany their Portuguese-American friend Isabel Sarmento and her father to Lisbon, Portugal. Senhor Sarmento has enlisted the assistance of the teen-age sister detectives in solving the baffling thefts of cork products from his Lisbon warehouse.

But even before the ocean liner *Balaska* leaves New York Harbor, Louise and Jean find themselves involved in a mystery on shipboard. What is the secret of the minstrel's magic music? Why is a thief so eager to get hold of the handsome young man's guitar? Is the dangerous schemer somehow connected with the warehouse thefts?

Louise and Jean successfully combine sightseeing in beautiful, romantic Portugal with outwitting a tribe of sinister gypsies as they unravel this seemingly unsolvable double mystery.

"I am marked for death!" the minstrel said grimly

The *Dana Girls* Mystery Stories

THE SECRET
of the
MINSTREL'S
GUITAR

By Carolyn Keene

GROSSET & DUNLAP

Publishers   *New York*

CONTENTS

THE SECRET
OF THE
MINSTREL'S GUITAR

CHAPTER I

"Full Speed Ahead!"

"Isn't this an exciting send-off?" said Jean Dana.

The blond, pretty sixteen-year-old was leaning on the rail of the transatlantic liner *Balaska*, which was captained by her Uncle Ned.

"It certainly is," agreed Jean's seventeen-year-old, brunette sister Louise. "And a mystery for us to solve when we get to Portugal."

Below them on the dock was a cheering, waving crowd of well-wishers, and around the Danas a number of fellow passengers. Bells were ringing, the ship's great horn was bellowing, and musicians were playing in the distance.

It was past time for the ship to sail. The girls wondered why it was still at the pier.

Captain Dana, who stood next to them, answered the question. "Too bad. I guess our wandering minstrel, Gama Gomes, isn't going to arrive. We must leave now." With a smile he went off.

"I'm sorry Gama didn't make it," Jean spoke up. "He sounds fascinating."

The young minstrel, who had come to the United States from Portugal, had sailed to New York with their Uncle Ned a few months before. The captain had taken a liking to the young man and had introduced him to several musical friends. At once the minstrel had become a great favorite both as a singer and a guitarist.

"I hear it's rumored there's magic in his guitar!" Louise remarked.

The Danas turned to a girl of eighteen and her father, about fifty, who stood next to them. The girl, Isabel Sarmento, had raven hair which offset a smooth olive complexion. The man had a shock of reddish-black curly hair and deeply tanned skin. They were Portuguese-Americans and had recently become acquainted with Louise and Jean.

Senhor Sarmento owned a factory near Lisbon, where he manufactured various articles made of cork. Some were shipped to his New York warehouse to be distributed throughout the United States. Recently there had been shortages in the shipments from Lisbon, and he was making the trip to Portugal to investigate the matter.

When Isabel had told her father the Dana girls were amateur sleuths, he had at once asked them to go along. The Danas could enjoy an interesting sightseeing trip in Portugal, as well as help solve the mystery!

Since Louise and Jean were on spring vacation from school, the trip had been arranged. To their delight, Mrs. Crandall, the headmistress at Starhurst School, had recently announced that students on a trip which would add to their general knowledge would be granted more time. The Danas were taking advantage of this opportunity.

In a few minutes the gangplank was pulled back onto the dock and the great liner began to move into the Hudson River. After the din of last-minute good-bys had died away, the passengers quieted down.

Clearly, though not loudly, the Danas and their friends could hear two young men, standing nearby, talking in an unfamiliar language. Both seemed agitated and were gesticulating excitedly. One pointed an angry fist at the dock.

"I wonder what they're talking about," said Louise.

Isabel smiled. "They are speaking in Romany."

"You mean they're gypsies?" Jean asked.

"Not necessarily," Isabel replied. "I learned a little of the gypsy language in my childhood in Portugal. The men are disturbed about the passenger who missed the boat. One of them said, 'This will spoil all the tree plans.'"

"Tree plans?" Jean repeated. "What in the world does that mean?"

"In Romany," Isabel whispered, "the word for tree is *ruk*. You figure it out."

Jean giggled. "Give me time."

Senhor Sarmento decided to go to his cabin and told the girls he would see them later. Soon the crowd dispersed, but Louise, Jean, and Isabel decided to wait on C deck while a special pilot guided the ship through the Narrows. There he would be picked up by a tug and taken ashore.

Half an hour later Louise sang out, "Here it comes!"

Shearing through the water was a sturdy but sleek tugboat. Signal blasts from the whistles of the big and small craft were exchanged as the tug drew alongside the *Balaska*.

"Girls, look!" Jean exclaimed suddenly. "That must be the missing minstrel, Gama Gomes, aboard!"

The dark-haired, slender musician of medium height had emerged from a small doorway onto the deck of the tug. He held his guitar case in one hand, a suitcase in the other.

"Isn't he handsome?" Isabel murmured dreamily.

Gama Gomes waited until the pilot had climbed down the Jacob's ladder from the *Balaska* and swung onto the tug. The singer had laid down the guitar case while waiting. Before he had a chance to climb the rope ladder, one of the Romany-speaking men scooted down it.

"I'll take care of this," he said, picking up the guitar.

"He's trying to steal the guitar!" Jean cried out

"Oh, thank you," Gomes murmured. He pulled himself up the ladder and set his suitcase on the deck. Then he turned and leaned over the rail, waiting for the other man to come up.

But the other man did not try to ascend. Without looking up, the Romany-speaking passenger shouted to the captain of the tugboat:

"Full speed ahead, sir!"

"What's that?" the officer shouted.

"I said, 'Take off!' "

The Danas were aghast and Jean cried out, "He's trying to steal the guitar!"

By this time the tugboat captain's face was livid. "I'm not taking orders from you or anyone else!" he shouted. "You and that guitar get back on the *Balaska* and be quick!"

The dark-haired man's face broke into a sneering smile. "Okay. Okay. What is the hurry? I am going. I only meant you could leave now—as soon as I was aboard."

Grasping the guitar, he climbed leisurely to the deck of the liner and Gama Gomes reached out to take the instrument.

"Thank you," he said, then walked off.

The tugboat gave a departing signal and chugged off.

"Now what do you make of that?" Louise asked, puzzled.

"I'd say the Romany-speaking fellow needs

watching," Jean answered. "I don't believe his explanation of why he told the tugboat captain to take off."

Isabel looked disgusted. "You really think he intended to steal the guitar? But how could he hope to get away with it?"

An elderly man who stood nearby smiled. "A thief is rarely prudent and often acts on the spur of the moment," he said.

Louise and Jean nodded. Then Louise said to Isabel and Jean, "Let's try to find the minstrel and talk to him. Maybe the two men know each other."

The girls spent twenty minutes trying to locate Gama, but the guitarist had disappeared.

"We'll see him later," Louise remarked. "Uncle Ned said he was going to ask him to play with the band tonight up in the dance lounge."

Isabel bubbled. "I've heard several of his records. Aren't they super?"

"Positively haunting," Jean answered. "You know, I can almost believe his guitar has magical powers. It sounds so different from any other."

The sisters wondered whether or not Uncle Ned knew of the incident and decided to talk to him right away. They invited Isabel to come.

"I'd love to," she said, "but first I want to check on my dad." She smiled. "I usually help him with packing and unpacking his clothes. Let's stop at his cabin."

The girls climbed the stairs again and followed Isabel to Senhor Sarmento's cabin. Isabel knocked on the door. Receiving no answer, she turned the knob and walked in.

A moment later Isabel gave a shriek. The Danas rushed inside.

CHAPTER II

Surprising Clue

"WHAT is it? What happened?" Louise cried out.

Isabel stood transfixed beside her father's bed. Senhor Sarmento lay sprawled out on it, unconscious.

"Dad!" Isabel cried out finally. "What happened to you?"

Louise moved forward and lifted the man's wrist. His pulse was very weak.

"He'll be all right, Isabel," Louise said, trying to be reassuring. "We must phone the ship's doctor. Jean, will you put in the call?"

Near the bed was a wall telephone. Jean quickly dialed the physician's quarters. A nurse, whom the girls knew from previous trips, answered and Jean identified herself.

"Hello, Jean. What's up?"

"Will you please ask Dr. Stanton if he can come

at once to Senhor Sarmento's cabin?" Jean asked. "He's unconscious."

"Oh!" the nurse said. "I'll tell the doctor right away."

Five minutes later Dr. Stanton appeared carrying his medical bag. He greeted the Danas and was introduced to Isabel.

At once Louise said, "Shall we girls wait outside?"

"Perhaps you'd better," he answered. "I'll talk to you after I've made an examination."

As soon as the girls reached the corridor, Isabel began to pace up and down. She wrung her hands, ran her fingers through her hair, and sobbed softly.

Louise and Jean kept pace with her, uttering words of encouragement. Their agitated companion did not seem to hear them.

"Oh, my precious father!" she murmured. "I hope—I fervently hope—that he isn't going to die!"

Louise spoke a bit sternly. "You must not have such dreadful thoughts," she said. "Think only that your father is going to get well."

Isabel squeezed her friend's hand. "You are right. If my dad is ill, he will need me and I must be strong."

Jean patted Isabel's arm. "That's better."

The girl's pacing was interrupted as the cabin door opened. Dr. Stanton motioned for them to come inside.

He said to Isabel, "Your father is going to be all right. Someone struck him on the head and he will be unconscious for a while. I think it best that he be removed to the infirmary."

The physician went to the telephone and requested that a stretcher be brought to the cabin. Then he turned to Isabel, "Has your father an enemy on board?"

Isabel looked startled. "If he has, we do not know who it is." She told about the mystery of the stolen cork products and added, "Maybe it is someone connected with the thefts."

Captain Dana, who had received word about Senhor Sarmento from the doctor's nurse, arrived at the same moment as the stretcher-bearers. He was dismayed and alarmed over what had happened, and ordered that every protection be given Senhor Sarmento.

He turned to Isabel. "Your cabin is next to your father's. Right?"

As she nodded, he said, "Perhaps it is not safe for you to be there. Suppose you move in with Louise and Jean and use their emergency bunk."

The three girls were delighted with this arrangement and the steward was summoned to transfer Isabel's baggage. She herself insisted upon accompanying her father to the infirmary and staying with him.

She explained, "I want to be there when he regains consciousness."

"That is a very good idea," Captain Dana agreed.

After she had left with the doctor and the stretcher-bearers, Captain Dana turned to his nieces. "How about you girls hunting for clues to the intruder? In the meantime I'll get hold of our ship's detective, Matt Wilson, and have him make an investigation too."

He telephoned the detective's quarters and was told that Mr. Wilson would come down in a few minutes. A gloomy expression crossed the captain's face as he turned to his nieces. "Please excuse me now. I must attend to some other important matters," he said. "You will let me know if you find anything."

Louise and Jean nodded. They had already started to do some sleuthing of their own. Nothing seemed to have been disturbed and the girls concluded this meant the attack had happened as soon as Senhor Sarmento had entered the cabin.

"The man must have been behind the door, ready to jump him," Louise conjectured. She stepped forward to close the half-opened door.

"Look!" Jean cried.

On the floor lay a face mask!

Louise picked it up. "I'm sure this belongs to Senhor Sarmento's attacker," she said, examining the thin rubber mask carefully.

"But what was it doing on the floor?" Jean asked, puzzled.

"That's a good question, Sis. Maybe Senhor Sarmento will have an answer."

"You mean there might have been a struggle and Senhor Sarmento pulled the mask off the attacker?" Jean was excited.

"Exactly." At that moment Louise bent over, then got down on her hands and knees.

"See something?" Jean asked.

Louise held up a small tuft of slightly wavy black hair as she arose. "This might be a clue. It's not the color of Senhor Sarmento's hair, and I'm sure the floor was vacuumed before passengers came aboard."

"But why would the intruder—?" Jean was saying when a uniformed officer walked into the cabin.

"Oh, hello, Mr. Wilson," Louise greeted him. "Have we got something to show you!" She displayed the hair and Jean handed him the mask. The girls related their suspicions of what had happened in the cabin.

"Senhor Sarmento may have grabbed his attacker's hair," Louise surmised.

"You could be right," Mr. Wilson said, then added, "We'd better not let anyone else in here."

He called the steward to lock the stateroom, then suggested he and the girls go to the infirmary. To everyone's relief, Senhor Sarmento had regained consciousness. Though extremely weak, he had managed to tell Isabel just what had taken place that afternoon.

As Senhor Sarmento had entered his room, he had heard a noise behind the door and wheeled around to face a masked man. The intruder hit him and Senhor Sarmento fell forward, at the same time grasping his assailant's mask. A second blow had sent the senhor reeling toward the bed and knocked him out. Detective Wilson produced the disguise.

"Yes, that's it," Senhor Sarmento said weakly.

"Could you identify him?" Louise asked.

"No. It was too sudden."

"Did you, by any chance, pull the man's hair?" Jean said.

"Why, yes, I did. But after that I don't remember anything."

Mr. Wilson was pleased with the Danas' clues. He put the telltale hairs in an envelope.

"I suppose you girls know," he said, "that hairs are practically as reliable an identification as fingerprints are. The structure of everyone's hair is different." After a pause he added, "There are over five hundred men on this ship. Matching these hairs with one of them is not going to be easy. If you girls come up with any feasible way to do this, let me know."

"We'll try hard to think of something," Louise promised. As the detective left, she thought, "Here is the kind of challenge Jean and I like!"

In the meantime, Senhor Sarmento had dropped

off to sleep. The Danas and Isabel tiptoed into the doctor's office. Isabel explained that her father was much better now. "But if you don't mind, I think I will stay here for a while."

"Don't forget to come to the boat drill," Jean told her. "That is compulsory."

"I'll be there. What's my station? I suppose now it will be the same as yours."

"It's number one," Jean replied. "Well, see you later."

As the Danas walked back to their own room, Jean spoke up. "I wish we could have cheered up Uncle Ned. He really looked quite upset."

"I'm afraid the only way to cheer him is to find out who attacked Senhor Sarmento," Louise answered. She paused briefly, then added, "During the boat drill all the passengers are required to be on deck—"

"Guess we're on the same wave length," Jean interrupted, winking at her sister. "Let's go talk to Uncle Ned right away."

The girls went to his quarters on the top deck and Louise told him their idea.

"The boat drill might be a good time to spot men with hair that looks like the sample," she said.

The captain's face brightened. "Very good," he said. "I'll tell you what we'll do. You report to your station when the gong sounds. I and my staff will come there first. Mr. Wilson will be with me.

After our inspection of number one station, suppose you girls follow us as we go from place to place."

The girls went to their own cabin and waited, eager to begin the next phase of their sleuthing. The summons for the boat drill was sounded a short time later. Louise and Jean hurried to the upper deck.

CHAPTER III

The Keepsake

ON THE way to the upper deck, Jean Dana suddenly burst into giggles.

"What's so funny?" Louise asked.

"I was just thinking," Jean said, "suppose we do find the suspect. What'll we do—snip off some of his hair?"

Louise laughed. "Not a bad idea, only how would we go about it and did you bring a pair of scissors with you?"

"I wish I had. I wouldn't mind trying," Jean answered.

A thought came to Louise. "Do you know who could help us? The barber. There's a chance the suspect will go there at least once during the trip."

"You're right. After the boat drill let's ask him."

By this time the girls had reached the upper deck and went at once to the number one station. A group of friendly, chattering men and women of various ages were waiting for the lifesaving drill. Each one had brought a life jacket from his cabin as required. Presently an officer and a crewman arrived.

First the officer instructed his listeners how to adjust the life jacket and a crewman assisted those who were having difficulty. Then the officer said:

"In case of emergency, you will stay here until instructed to go to a lifeboat. When the signal is given, you will march orderly to climb aboard. It is an old rule of the sea that women and children go first."

He smiled. "Remember, do not panic. That only causes confusion and delays lifesaving operations. I am sure you will have no cause for worry on this trip. Weather predictions are for clear skies and unseasonably warm temperatures. In a few minutes Captain Dana and two of the ship's officers will come for inspection. Please stay here until you have been dismissed."

While waiting, Louise and Jean scrutinized each of the men in the group. Not one had hair resembling the sample.

Uncle Ned and the two officers arrived within a few minutes. The group at number one station passed inspection and was dismissed. As Captain Dana proceeded to the next station, Louise and Jean fell into step behind the officers, who stopped a short distance away.

There were more men in this group than in the previous one. Again the girls' eyes roved over the crowd. At first disappointed, Louise suddenly spotted one young man whose slightly wavy black hair certainly made him a suspect.

The man was Gama Gomes the minstrel!

The girls exchanged amazed glances. It had never dawned on them that a friend of Uncle Ned's might be guilty! What should they do now?

By this time Captain Dana had finished his inspection and the passengers were allowed to leave.

"We'd better follow Uncle Ned," Louise whispered to Jean. "There may be other possible suspects."

"I guess you're right," Jean answered. "But I'm certainly curious to find out about Gama, aren't you?"

"I sure am. Suppose we ask Uncle Ned what we'd better do."

She ran up to him and whispered her secret. He thought a moment, then said, "You work on this clue as best you can. I'll keep my eyes open for anyone whose hair looks like Gama's."

Louise and Jean hurried back to their cabin to remove the life jackets. Isabel was not there and they assumed she had returned to the infirmary to see her father.

"Just how do we follow through on this lead, Sis?" Jean asked in a mock professional tone.

"Let's talk to the barber first, then try to find

Senhor Gomes again," Louise proposed. "We may be able to get a sample of his hair." She paused a moment. "I must admit, I feel a little silly doing this."

Jean nodded. "I know just what you mean. If I didn't think it was going to lead us literally within a hairsbreadth of the villain, I don't think I'd have the courage to go on."

The ship's barber had nearly finished with a customer when the Danas walked into the shop. They waited until the gray-haired man had paid for his haircut and left, then made their request. Somewhat reluctantly, the barber agreed to save any black wavy hair clippings in separate envelopes marked with the customers' names and send them to Officer Wilson.

The Danas thanked him and hurried to Gama Gomes's cabin. The minstrel was strumming his guitar when they knocked. Louise and Jean introduced themselves.

With a beguiling smile, Gama said, "Your uncle told me about you girls when I first came over on this ship to America. He is very fond of you and thinks you are so bright and clever."

Both girls blushed and at once Jean said, "The admiration is mutual. Our uncle has told us he thinks you're one of the finest musicians in the world."

Gama Gomes laughed. "That is a lot to live up to. Would you like to hear a couple of songs?"

"Oh yes!"

The minstrel motioned the girls to chairs. Then he stood in front of them and began to play. The tune, unfamiliar to them, was very beautiful. As Gama strummed his guitar, haunting sounds issued from it. There were distinct overtones like a faint echo or a second guitarist in a duet.

When the minstrel finished, he began to play the whole number over again. This time he sang. The Danas could not understand the words, but recognized their resemblance to Romany.

At the end the girls clapped and Louise remarked, "The song is lovely. What is the name of it?"

Gama Gomes smiled. "I call it, 'Love Is an Endless Circle.' "

"You mean you wrote it?" Jean asked quickly.

The minstrel nodded. "I expect to make a recording of it when I return to the United States."

Louise spoke up. "Are the words in Romany?"

"Yes."

The girls gave him a searching look. "Senhor Gomes, are you a gypsy?"

He gave her a flashing smile. "Yes, I am. My queen gave me this guitar when I left. She said she had put a magic spell on it."

"The music that comes out is certainly magic," Louise conceded.

The minstrel asked if either of the girls played the guitar. Both said they had taken a few lessons.

"Would you like to try mine?" he asked.

"May I?" Jean said eagerly. She jumped up and took the instrument. Sitting down again, she examined the guitar more closely. "This is unlike any I have ever seen," she remarked.

Gama Gomes said it was a Portuguese guitar, very different from those in Spain. "You'll note," he said, "that it has twelve strings in pairs of six. And the soundbox is round at the base."

Jean plucked a few strings, then began to play a simple melody. When she finished, Gama Gomes praised her. "You would become an excellent player if you practiced a lot," he said.

Louise took her turn and received the same praise. The sisters vowed that they would practice in earnest after they returned to school.

As Louise handed the instrument back to the minstrel, she said, "Thank you very much." Lowering her eyes, she added coyly, "Please don't think me a silly teen-ager, but I'd like to ask a favor of you."

"What is it?" Gama Gomes asked.

"I would love to have a real keepsake. Would it be possible for me to have a lock of your hair?"

Jean had difficulty keeping her face straight. Under ordinary circumstances such a request would be the last thing in the world Louise would make of a celebrity!

Gama Gomes did not seem the least bit startled

by the request. "I am flattered," he said. "Of course you may have a lock of my hair." He walked over to a shelf on which lay a shaving kit. He opened it and took out a small pair of scissors.

Looking in the mirror, he contemplated where he would cut his hair. He finally chose a spot on the back of his head, then picked up an envelope and dropped the hairs inside. With a laugh he grabbed a pen and signed his name on the envelope.

"Oh, this is wonderful!" Louise said, feeling a little guilty that she suspected this affable young man. He most certainly did not look like a villain! She reflected. "How could a villain write such a beautiful love song? And why would such a famous singer attack Senhor Sarmento?"

After the girls left the minstrel's cabin, they headed at once for Matt Wilson's office. They found him in his laboratory with Dr. Stanton, reading Senhor Sarmento's X-rays. Isabel was with them eagerly awaiting their findings.

The three greeted the Danas, then Dr. Stanton said, "I'm happy to report that Senhor Sarmento does not have a skull fracture. He is lucky, because he did receive a hard blow, probably with a fist."

The relief on Isabel's face was almost pathetic. Louise and Jean hugged her, saying how happy they were at the news.

"And now, Miss Sarmento," said Dr. Stanton, "your father wants you to spend time with the girls and have some fun. Everything will be all right. It is not necessary for you to spend every minute with him."

At first Isabel demurred, but Louise and Jean urged her to follow the doctor's advice.

"Before we leave," Louise said to Mr. Wilson, "we want to give you a clue that ought to help."

"You mean to Senhor Sarmento's attacker?"

"Yes. Jean and I have started trying to find the person whose hair matches the sample you have." She brought the envelope from her pocket. "I honestly believe that this one is not going to match, though."

Jean said, "And I fervently hope not. Gama Gomes is too nice a person to be involved in such a mess."

"Gama Gomes?" Isabel repeated. "Oh, how dreadful if he's the one!"

Matt Wilson said he would settle the matter at once. He asked the girls to sit down while he examined the two envelopes of hair under the microscope in his laboratory. Though it was only a short time before he returned to the anxious girls, it seemed endless. They fidgeted and walked the floor.

When the detective appeared, his face broke into a smile. "Have no further fears," he said. "Your friend Senhor Gomes has hair texture quite different from the villain you are seeking."

"Thank goodness!" Jean burst out.

Matt Wilson laughed. "Keep up the good work. When may I look for some more hair samples?"

"Any time," Louise answered. "Maybe tomorrow. We've asked the barber to help us." The girls giggled and left the laboratory.

That evening after dinner there was to be a concert in the ballroom preceding the dance. The girls went early to get front seats. The band arrived promptly. After playing one number, the leader announced a piano solo, to be followed by another band selection.

Finally Gama Gomes was introduced. Well known by reputation, the popular young musician received an ovation. Some teen-agers began to squeal and the young gypsy smiled broadly and waved to them.

"Thank you. Thank you," he said, but the words were drowned out by the applause.

"Please, please," Gomes begged, and finally the teen-age enthusiasts became quiet.

He played several songs and ended with the original composition he had sung for the girls that morning. But this time he sang the words in Portuguese. Was it possible he did not want the public to know he was a gypsy?

When the concert ended, small tables were set up around the perimeter of the room and the chairs put in place. Isabel and the Danas found a table.

It was not long before three young men approached their table and without being invited sat down. The girls recognized one of them as the passenger who had climbed down to the tugboat to get Gama Gomes's guitar. "My name is Sylvestre Diogo," he said.

"And mine is Garcia Torres," another spoke up. For the first time the girls noticed that both men had slightly wavy black hair and at once suspicion was directed at them.

The third man, Alfredo Moreira, was a blond Portuguese. All the girls liked him at once but did not care for Torres and Diogo.

The dance music started and at once Alfredo claimed Isabel as a partner. The Danas were not eager to dance with the other men, but saw no way of avoiding it. Diogo swept Jean onto the floor, while Torres grabbed Louise's hand and pulled her toward him.

It was soon evident that he was a crude dancer. He held his partner too tightly and did not keep in step with the music. Louise thought, "I must find some excuse to sit down. I can't stand this."

They passed the band, and were circling back toward their table, when suddenly Torres gave Louise a tremendous hug. At the same time he hissed into her ear, "Would you marry a gypsy?"

CHAPTER IV

Warning Symbol

To herself Louise said, "You obnoxious man!"

She did not reply to Torres at once, and pulled away from him as much as possible. Finally she said, "Why do you ask such a question?"

Torres gave a wide grin. "Because I think that gypsy guitarist is in love with you."

"What nonsense!" Louise exclaimed.

"I know I am right. And besides, you are in love with him," Torres announced.

Louise was almost too shocked to reply. What was this man getting at? She wanted to tell him she was leaving, but decided she had better find out all she could.

"You are talking utter foolishness," she said, "but tell me what makes you think such a thing."

Torres laughed. "Didn't you ask the minstrel for a lock of his hair?"

Louise wondered how Torres knew about it.

Had Gomes told him—or had Torres overheard them talking in the minstrel's cabin?

She said, "You mean if a girl is in love with a man, it is a gypsy custom that she ask him for a lock of hair?"

Her partner did not answer the question directly. Instead he said, "You have a lot to learn about gypsies, young lady. For one thing, did you know that Gama Gomes is an outcast—a *marimé*—from his tribe?"

"I know nothing about Gama Gomes except that he plays the guitar very well and has a nice singing voice," Louise answered icily.

Torres went on gloatingly, "Do you know Gama Gomes is not his real name?"

"Most people in the entertainment world take assumed names," the girl countered.

By this time she and her partner were nearing the table where they had been seated. She stopped dancing abruptly and said, "Thank you for the dance. I'm going to sit down now."

Torres was not to be put off this easily. He followed her to the table and dropped into a chair. "I want to give you a friendly warning. Watch out for Gama Gomes. He is not what he appears to be. He's a bad man."

Torres lapsed into silence as the other two men came back to the table with Isabel and Jean. Both girls had noticed Louise's unpleasant experience on the dance floor and knew that she wanted to leave. Isabel said, "I must go now and see my father. Are you girls coming?"

The Danas jumped up quickly and Jean said, "Indeed we are."

The three girls said good night to the men and hurried off. On the way to the infirmary, Jean and Isabel demanded to know what had happened. When they heard the story they were shocked.

"I believe everything was made up," Jean declared. "Isabel, did you ever hear of a custom where a girl asks for a lock of hair because she's in love with a man?"

"No, I never did. And it is difficult for me to believe that Gama Gomes is a bad man."

Louise said, "I wonder what Torres's reason was for telling me such a thing."

"Search me," Jean replied. "But I think we ought to find out. I am still wondering why Gama sang 'Endless Circle' in Portuguese instead of in Romany. There may be some truth to Torres's story after all."

Louise mentioned that both Torres and Diogo had slightly wavy black hair very similar to the sample Mr. Wilson was holding. She smiled. "I wouldn't dare ask either one of them to cut off a lock so I can make a comparison!"

Jean said cheerfully, "Maybe the barber will have some hair clippings tomorrow."

The girls were delighted to find Senhor Sarmento feeling better. They wished him a good night's sleep and departed to their cabin.

The following morning when Louise, Jean, and Isabel were on their way to breakfast they passed Gama Gomes's door. It was slightly ajar, and they could see him seated on his bed, his head in his hands.

The Danas paused and Louise knocked. The minstrel looked up. He did not smile and there was a very sad expression on his face.

"Good morning, Senhor Gomes," Louise said. "Is something the matter?"

The guitarist stood up and walked to the door.

"Good morning, Miss Dana. Yes, something very dreadful is the matter." He pointed to three symbols which had been crayoned onto the door.

"What do they mean?" asked Jean, staring at the marks. They looked like:

$$\mathcal{H} \, \mathsf{d} \, \mathsf{H}$$

"How strange!" said Isabel. "What do they mean?"

The minstrel tightened his fist and his lips were grim. "The first means person, the second house, and the third sword. They say that I am marked for death!"

"Oh!" the three girls cried out. "How dreadful!"

Louise asked if these were gypsy symbols.

The guitarist nodded. "I was not aware that there were any other gypsies aboard the *Balaska*," he said, "but evidently there is at least one."

Jean said that they knew of at least two other men who spoke Romany. "Their names are Garcia Torres and Sylvestre Diogo. It was Diogo who tried to steal your guitar. Did you ever hear of these men?"

"No, and those are not gypsy names."

Louise wondered whether the girls should say any more about the men at this time, but decided against it. She came to the conclusion that either Torres or Diogo was undoubtedly a suspect, not only of having scratched the symbols on the door but also of having attacked Senhor Sarmento. Now Gama's life was in danger!

"You should not stay here alone," Louise told the guitarist.

"I am not afraid," he replied quickly.

Jean and Isabel tried to make him realize the danger but he brushed off their warnings.

Finally Jean said, "Would you be willing to let Captain Dana make the decision? In any case, he certainly should be told about the symbols and what they mean."

"I suppose you are right," Gomes finally conceded. "I will tell him sometime today."

Louise felt they should not wait a minute longer. She explained to Gama that the captain was responsible for everything and everyone on shipboard and no one should withhold vital information about the mystery from him.

"Please come with us now. I am sure he will be in his quarters," Jean urged.

Reluctantly the minstrel consented. He locked the cabin door and followed the girls.

Uncle Ned Dana was just about to order breakfast brought to him. Usually he ate at the captain's table in the large dining room, but when he was pressed for time, he had meals served in his cabin. At the moment he was working on navigational charts.

"Good morning, girls," he said heartily. "Gama, I'm glad to see you. Something important must be in the wind to bring you here so early."

"Important and serious," Louise told him.

The story of the symbols and their dire meaning was quickly told. Captain Dana frowned deeply. "Serious indeed," he said. "Gama, have you any idea who put the marks on your door?"

"Unfortunately no. I did not know I had enemies on board, least of all anyone who wants to kill me."

The captain rubbed his chin thoughtfully. Finally he said, "It is certainly not safe for you to stay in your cabin. Please remain right here and bunk with me. I'll have two breakfasts sent up."

"Thank you, sir," the guitarist said. "But first I must go back to my cabin and pack my clothes and get my guitar."

"Just a minute," said Captain Dana. "My nieces can ask your room steward to do the packing, and your bag can be brought up here secretly."

"And may I bring up the guitar?" Louise asked.

"Hope Torres didn't hear you say that," Jean said teasingly. Her sister blushed.

"Hm! What's this about Torres again?" Gama asked, puzzled.

Louise hesitated a moment, then related part of her conversation with the suspect. "Last night at the dance he mentioned the lock of hair I asked you for—"

Before she could continue, Gama interrupted. "How did he know of that?" The minstrel bit his lip nervously. "He must have been eavesdropping."

"Or perhaps he simply overheard my request as he was walking past your cabin," Louise put in quickly. She hoped to allay Gama Gomes's fears. Jean, catching on, nodded in agreement.

Gama smiled. "You are quite right. I must not be so suspicious of everything. Please forgive me." Then he added, "My answer to your original question, Louise, is, of course, you may bring up my guitar. I would not trust the instrument to many people but I know you will guard it carefully."

The three girls started down to the minstrel's cabin. While they were still some distance up the corridor, Isabel exclaimed, "Look!"

The girls could hardly believe what they saw. A dark-haired man with an ugly face was just coming out of Gama's cabin. In one hand he carried a guitar case.

"Gama's guitar!" Jean cried out. "That man's stealing it!"

The girls ran as fast as they could. The thief, hearing footsteps behind him, looked over his shoulder and quickened his pace. Then, realizing he was being pursued, he started to run.

CHAPTER V

The Gypsy's Story

As the fleeing thief reached a corner of the dimly lighted corridor, he ran smack into a steward with a tray of breakfast. Dishes of food crashed to the floor.

Both the steward and the man with the guitar teetered to regain their balances. In the mix-up the instrument slid from the thief's hand.

By this time the Dana girls had reached the spot. Quick as a wink Jean grabbed up the guitar case and ran in the opposite direction before the stranger could take it again.

The thief knew he was cornered. Instead of arguing, he jumped across the dishes and food and sped off. Louise was right on his heels.

"I never saw him before," she thought. "I wonder who he is."

Within seconds the thief turned from the main

corridor into a shorter one, on both sides of which there were cabins. By the time Louise reached the area, the man was out of sight.

"He must have gone into one of the staterooms," she decided. "But which one?"

She thought of knocking on each door but decided against this. The thief certainly would not answer her knock.

"I could ask the purser who the people are that occupy all these cabins," she thought. "But while I'm gone, the man will vanish again."

It occurred to her that since she had not seen him before, and he was a thief, he might have been wearing a disguise—a rubber mask. If so, he could reappear presently looking like someone else.

"I'll wait around for a little while, anyhow," Louise decided.

She walked up and down the main corridor for twenty minutes but no one reappeared. Finally Louise gave up and returned to her own cabin.

Jean, sitting there with Isabel, explained that she had delivered the guitar to Gama. The steward would bring up his clothing later on. Both girls were eager to hear Louise's story.

She related what had happened, and added, "I think that thief was wearing a disguise."

"I'm glad," said Isabel, "that the guitar was rescued. It would have been dreadful if we had had to tell Gama it was gone. What do we do now?"

"Talk to Detective Wilson," Louise replied.

The man was in his office and greeted the girls affably. "I'm glad you came. What's on your mind?"

When Louise and Jean finished relating their recent adventure, the officer wrinkled his brow. "Thank goodness you got the guitar away from that man. But I'm sorry he vanished."

Matt Wilson said he would find out who occupied the cabins in the corridor where the suspected thief had disappeared.

"He was such a funny-looking person, I suspect he was wearing a disguise," Louise said.

"In that case I may even have the rooms searched," the detective declared.

He went off at once. But when the girls met him later on, he admitted that nothing had come of his investigation. Among the occupants of the cabins in that corridor there was only one man. He was elderly, gray-haired, and well known to Captain Dana.

"The thief must have had a key to one of the cabins and hid in there temporarily," Wilson said.

He also had another idea. "If we don't catch the attacker or the thief—I'm inclined to think he may be the same person—I can order all the baggage searched when it goes through customs."

Jean smiled. "You mean you'll find the mask and maybe a wig?"

"Yes."

"But," Jean went on, "if this man is as clever as

he appears to be, don't you think he'd drop them overboard before we dock?"

The detective thought this over a moment. "You're probably right," he conceded.

"We're very suspicious of two men named Torres and Diogo," Jean revealed. "We think they may be gypsies."

"Yes," Louise added. "They seem a little too interested in Gama and his guitar, but I don't know how we'll ever get samples of their hair!"

Matt Wilson smiled. "I've ordered every room steward to bring me samples of any black hair they find in the rooms. But I'd appreciate your bringing me some too! I haven't heard from the barber."

Louise and Jean spent most of the afternoon trying to pick up further clues. Dinnertime came without their having learned anything. After dinner they attended a movie.

Before going to bed, Louise said, "I wonder how everything is up in Uncle Ned's quarters. Let's go and see him." She had not mentioned Gama Gomes's name in case someone were listening.

The stairway to the top deck had been roped off and a sign hung across it:

No Passengers Allowed Beyond This Point

Giggling, the Danas and Isabel crouched under the heavy chain and climbed the iron steps. As they reached the top deck, Isabel exclaimed, "What a gorgeous moon!"

It seemed to hang lazily over the water and cast a soft white glow across the deck. Ship's lanterns were shining here and there and lights were on in the deckhouse. Jean knocked and the door was opened.

Gama Gomes was there alone. The young man said he was very glad to see the girls because he had been lonesome. "I haven't even been playing my guitar," he said dolefully.

To cheer him up, Louise said, "How about playing it for us now? Why don't we go out on deck and you can play to us softly?"

The gypsy's eyes sparkled. "I would love to do that. Suppose you wait for me outside."

The girls stepped back onto the deck and again gazed at the moon. It occurred to them Gama was taking a long time and wondered if he had changed his mind. Presently they heard him come outside and gasped in astonishment. He was wearing a gypsy costume and looked very much the part of a minstrel.

"Senhor Gomes," said Isabel, "you are even more handsome in your gypsy costume than you are in your American clothes."

The guitarist laughed, then began to play.

"First a little song about moonlight," he said and began to strum softly.

The girls recognized "Moon on the Mississippi" and hummed it quietly. As the song ended, Isabel suddenly looked toward a stack of chairs.

"I thought I heard a noise over there," she whispered.

The others gazed at the stacked chairs but could see nothing, and concluded no one was around.

"Let's sit down," Louise suggested.

They all dropped to the deck. Gomes's back was to the captain's cabin. The three girls were arranged in a semicircle before him and listened in rapt attention as he continued to play and sing. Some of the words were in Romany, others in Portuguese, and a few in English.

"You are very talented," Louise said.

Before he had a chance to reply, footsteps echoed on the iron stairway and in a moment Captain Dana appeared. His face was stern.

"Gama," he said, "you are not supposed to leave the cabin. Now we will all go inside. You are not to play the guitar again. It attracts attention to your hiding place."

He took the instrument from the musician and motioned everyone into his quarters. Captain Dana disappeared into his bedroom and the others assumed he was locking up the instrument.

The minstrel looked crestfallen. Jean realized how much the guitar meant to him. To offset his gloomy spirits, she said, "Would you like to tell us about your life?"

The guitarist thought a moment, then a smile crossed his face. "It is a strange story," he said, "but if you want to listen, I will be glad to tell you."

"Please do," the girls begged as Captain Dana reappeared.

Suddenly Gama Gomes grinned boyishly. "Did you ever hear of a reformed gypsy?" he asked.

The girls did not answer. They merely smiled and urged him to go on.

"When I was a little boy," he said, "I was not allowed to go to school. I was taught how to play the guitar, how to handle horses, and—and how to steal."

"Oh!" Isabel gasped. "Is that all you were taught?"

"That is all. But then a change came. When I was about twelve years old," the gypsy went on, "a kindly old man wandered into our camp and begged a meal. I talked to him and in a whisper he said he would teach me secretly to read and write. I was to meet him under a nearby cork tree."

The minstrel went on to say that he was an apt pupil and the old man followed the tribe for years. "I sneaked food to him and in return he taught me like a teacher—and like a minister. After a while I began to see that stealing was wrong.

"When I was eighteen years old, I was completely converted and felt that my tribe should be also. One evening I stood up at a council meeting of our Ker tribe and said so. What an uproar there was!"

"I'll bet!" Jean remarked. "Then what happened?"

The gypsy said he was given a trial at the Romany Kris. "That is our court. The verdict was that I should be banished forever!"

The girls were too amazed to speak. There was some truth to Torres's story!

Gama Gomes went on, "Our Queen Tekla felt sorry for me. She could not change the verdict, but she gave me a marvelous present when I left. This guitar! She said she had put a spell of magic on it.

"And this is true! I went to the United States and have made a fair amount of money with my playing and singing. Unfortunately, most of the money was stolen in New York." The minstrel paused. Then he added sadly, "Now someone on this ship is threatening me and trying to steal my guitar!"

There was a moment of silence after this statement. Then just outside the captain's quarters there was a tremendous crash!

CHAPTER VI

The Ransacked Cabin

THE Danas and their companions rushed out of the captain's quarters and looked around. A pile of deck chairs near the cabin had toppled over.

Louise and Jean wondered whether the stack had fallen by itself or had been pushed. At the same moment the two girls spotted a man running down the iron stairway. They rushed over to get a better glimpse of him, but by the time they reached the steps, he had disappeared.

"Louise, he must have been eavesdropping while hiding behind the stack of chairs!" Jean exclaimed.

"Yes, and heard everything we said. Now he knows where Gama Gomes and his guitar are hidden!"

The girls turned to Captain Dana and Louise said she thought Gama should change his hiding place and that of his guitar.

Gomes spoke up. "But where can I go? Every place I've been, someone finds me."

"I think the best place for you to hide," said Captain Dana, "is among the band musicians. You'd better go down there this very night. Take the guitar with you and don't come out of those quarters until I tell you."

The captain then turned to his nieces and Isabel. "You girls go down first. If you see anyone lurking on the stairways, come back to warn us. Gama and I will follow in a few minutes. I think it best if we wrap the guitar case in a blanket."

Captain Dana gave the girls directions to the musicians' quarters four decks down and said the cabin door was marked *Private. Rehearsal Room.*

Scooting down one stairway after another, Isabel and Louise followed Jean's lead. No one had passed them and they were hopeful this time that Gama Gomes would really be safe from his enemy.

The following morning the Danas decided to go for an early dip in the ship's pool. Isabel said she was too sleepy. To their disappointment they found there was no water in the pool, and a sign was posted to announce it would not open until ten o'clock.

"Before we go back to our cabin," Louise said, "let's say good morning to Uncle Ned."

The girls hurried up the stairway to the top deck and knocked on his door. There was no answer.

"You don't suppose he is still asleep?" Jean asked unbelievingly.

Louise laughed. "Not Uncle Ned. You know how early he always gets up."

The girls were about to turn away when both of them stopped short. They looked at each other and then began to grin.

"Fine detectives we are," Louise said. "The least we can do is find out if the door is open."

Before doing this, she pounded loudly on the panel. There was still no answer, so she tried the knob. The door opened. Louise gasped.

"Oh, my goodness!" she exclaimed, stepping inside.

The room was a shambles. Lockers were pulled open. Papers and records were strewn about.

The girls rushed into their uncle's bedroom. Similar damage had been done there. Clothes were flung everywhere, and the bed had been pulled apart.

"I wonder if anything was taken," Jean said. "And whether or not Uncle Ned knows about this. Maybe he rushed off to report the incident to Detective Wilson."

Louise did not answer. After some further thought, she said, "I'll bet the intruder was after Gama's guitar."

"You're right," Jean agreed. "We must find Uncle Ned at once."

Suddenly the sisters panicked. The same dire question struck both of them. Had Uncle Ned been in his room when the intruder came? The captain may have tangled with him and lost!

"Oh, Louise!" cried Jean, a catch in her voice. "Maybe Uncle Ned's been injured!"

"Or tossed—tossed overboard," Louise added fearfully.

The girls shivered in fright for a few seconds. Then Louise took a deep breath, went into the cabin's sitting room, and telephoned the purser. He had not seen the captain at all that morning! She related what had taken place and asked where her uncle might be.

"Down in the engine room perhaps."

The Danas hurried to the engineer's office, but the skipper had not been there. Next they talked to a dining-room steward. Again no luck.

"I have another guess," Jean said. "The infirmary. Uncle Ned may have gone to see Senhor Sarmento."

The girls hurried to Dr. Stanton's office. "It's not visiting hours yet." The doctor chuckled.

The sisters realized they were being teased, but there was no time for repartee. "This is an emergency!" Louise spluttered. "Have you seen the captain?"

"Yes. He is visiting Senhor Sarmento."

"We must speak to him at once. Uncle Ned's cabin has been ransacked."

"Oh, my goodness!" Louise exclaimed

"What!"

Dr. Stanton got up from his desk chair and went at once to tell Captain Dana, who appeared in moments. "Good morning, my hearties. What's this I hear about my quarters being ransacked?"

"It's true," Louise said quickly. "Jean and I came up to say good morning to you. When you didn't answer, we walked in."

"You walked in? But the door was locked!" the captain exclaimed in astonishment.

"I'm sorry, Uncle Ned," said Jean, "but the door was *not* locked and there were no signs it had been forced open. Please come with us and check to see if anything has been stolen."

He followed them to the top deck and rushed into his quarters. "What devil's been in here?" he boomed. The captain quickly began to search both the sitting room and bedroom. Finally he said, "So far as I can see, nothing seems to be missing, just mussed up."

"Jean and I believe the intruder was looking for Gama's guitar," Louise declared.

"Well, thank goodness we removed it," Uncle Ned replied. He smiled a little. "I see you girls are all set for a swim, but the pool isn't open yet and you probably haven't had any breakfast." He hesitated a moment, then asked, "How would you like to come up here after breakfast and do a little housekeeping?"

His nieces grinned and Jean answered, "How about if we eat later and do your housekeeping now? Then we'll have bigger appetites."

The captain smiled appreciatively. "You know how I hate untidiness and I never allow it on shipboard. I would like to see my room put in first-class order again."

He paused briefly, then added, "Maybe Matt Wilson should get up here and scout for clues."

Captain Dana summoned the detective, who arrived in a few minutes. The officer was astounded at the disarray.

"This was a thorough job all right," he commented.

He whipped a magnifying glass from a pocket and began looking for fingerprints. Was he also looking for telltale black hairs? the girls wondered. They themselves began to look for clues as they tidied up the cabin.

As Jean was about to make up the captain's bed, she spotted a rolled-up red handkerchief. "Is this yours, Uncle Ned?" she asked.

He came across the room to look. "No, I never saw it before."

"Possibly it belongs to Gama," Louise suggested. "It looks like a gypsy's scarf."

Captain Dana telephoned the musicians' suite and told the minstrel what had happened and asked about the scarf.

"No, it does not belong to me," the young guitarist replied.

Upon hearing this, Jean concluded, "Then it must belong to the intruder."

Louise took the handkerchief from her sister and began to unroll it. A small object slipped out and dropped to the floor.

CHAPTER VII

The Tip-off

EVERYONE in the captain's bedroom looked at the shiny object on the floor. It was a key. The detective picked it up.

After examining it, he said grimly, "It looks like a skeleton key!"

"So that's how Uncle Ned's visitor got in," Louise declared.

"I'm afraid so," Matt Wilson answered. "It proves we are not dealing with a small-time crook. He didn't find what he was looking for, so he'll be searching somewhere else."

Although the girls said nothing, they agreed with the detective's reasoning. But where would the slippery thief strike next?

As soon as Louise and Jean straightened up the captain's quarters, they left to dress for breakfast. While they were changing, Louise remarked, "Jean, since that red handkerchief we found looks like the kind gypsies use—"

"You mean," Jean interrupted, "it might belong to Torres or Diogo."

"Yes."

Jean suggested that after breakfast the girls try to learn where the two men had been early in the morning. Her sister made a wry face. "You know what that means? They'll probably try to make a date with us."

Before Jean could comment, their room telephone rang. Isabel quickly answered it. Alfredo and two American boys she had met at a friend's home in New York were asking for dates with the three girls. They suggested meeting at the swimming pool later, having lunch, and going to the dance that night.

Isabel covered the telephone receiver and whispered the names of the boys and their request. Jean and Louise accepted promptly, and thought, "If they only knew how relieved we are!"

After breakfast Isabel asked the Danas to accompany her to the infirmary to see her father. The three had barely arrived and seated themselves when a radiogram was handed to Senhor Sarmento. He tore it open, and as he read the message, he wrinkled his brow.

"Dad, what is it?" Isabel asked worriedly.

He handed her the radio message, which was in Portuguese. She read it quickly and gasped. Then she translated the message for the Danas.

The radiogram was from the manager of Senhor

Sarmento's cork company in Lisbon. There had been a large and recent theft at the dock warehouse. Furthermore, the company had received a tip that one or more members of the thieves' gang were aboard the *Balaska!*

"How dreadful!" Louise exclaimed.

"What do you make of it?" Senhor Sarmento asked the Danas.

At once Jean replied, "I'd say the person who attacked you may be one of the thieves."

Isabel's father said Captain Dana had already insisted that for reasons of safety, he remain in the infirmary until the end of the sea trip.

"I'm glad of that," said Louise.

Senhor Sarmento nodded sadly. "But this means that I cannot protect my daughter and I feel that she too is in danger."

Louise quickly assured Senhor Sarmento that they would take care of Isabel.

"I appreciate your kindness, but I am afraid I shall worry."

Louise tried to get the senhor's mind off his problems by discussing all they would do in Lisbon. Isabel took the cue and began to talk about the quaint fishing village of Nazaré some distance up the coast from the capital.

"You'll love the town," she said. "The women and girls dress so colorfully. Some wear as many as seven different petticoats!"

"And the fishermen have colorful clothes, too,"

Senhor Sarmento said. "They wear bright plaid jackets and tasseled stocking caps. The caps keep their heads warm and the tassels are used to store all sorts of things—pipes, tobacco, even valuables."

Isabel laughed. "Once, when I was a little girl, a fisherman called Goncalves told me of a voyage he and some fishing mates had taken. Their boat was driven by a windstorm to a mysterious island which had once been a pirate's hideout! Goncalves showed me an old gold piece he had found there. He kept it ever since in the tassel of his cap for good luck."

"How fascinating!" Jean commented.

Senhor Sarmento said he hoped the girls would have time to go to the Hall of Magpies in a palace at Sintra.

"Live magpies?" Louise asked.

"No," he replied. "They are painted in a circle on a ceiling in what was originally the queen's suite.

"There is a very amusing story connected with the place," said Senhor Sarmento. He laughed heartily. "It seems the king was fond of one of the ladies-in-waiting. One day the queen caught him kissing her and spread the story throughout the court. The king was so provoked, he said the queen and her ladies-in-waiting were a lot of gossipy magpies and ordered magpies painted on the ceiling of the queen's suite to remind them of that fact."

Louise and Jean laughed. "I wonder if his scheme stopped the gossip," Jean said.

Isabel giggled. "And I wonder if it kept the king from kissing other women."

The Danas thought Senhor Sarmento seemed tired now, so they stood up to leave. Isabel, however, decided to stay with her father for a while.

"I'll see you and the boys for lunch at the pool," she said.

On the way back to their cabin, Louise and Jean decided to stop at Matt Wilson's office to talk to the detective. He said there were no more clues to the matching of the suspect's hair. The detective was astounded by the radiogram message for Senhor Sarmento and admitted the whole matter was very baffling.

"We'll just have to work harder to find out who's responsible for all the mysterious happenings on the *Balaska*," Louise said.

As she and Jean walked along the corridor, Louise suggested they go to the cabin occupied by Torres and Diogo. "I don't like them, but we must find out if either of them is guilty."

"Right."

The steward who was tidying up the room told the girls that the men had gone up to the swimming pool. "Guess they'll be there all morning."

Jean suddenly squeezed Louise's hand as if to say, "Do you see what I see?"

On a wall shelf lay two solid-color handkerchiefs, very much like the one found in Captain Dana's bedroom!

The girls left the cabin and hurried up the corridor. Louise said with determination, "Now I'm more convinced than ever one or both is guilty. We must try to get samples of Torres's and Diogo's hair."

"I'm with you," Jean agreed.

Reaching their own stateroom, the Danas unlocked the cabin door and walked in. The curtains had been drawn. Before the girls could turn to close the door, it was quickly shut and locked behind them. Startled, Jean and Louise whirled.

An ugly, tousled-haired man was standing before them and leering menacingly. Before either girl could speak, he growled, "Where's the minstrel's guitar?"

Jean and Louise did not answer.

"You tell me where the guitar is," the man threatened, "or you'll regret it!"

CHAPTER VIII

The Intruder's Demand

STUNNED by the sudden turn of events, Louise and Jean stared fearfully at the intruder who had imprisoned them in their cabin. Both girls realized that their only hope of getting away from him was to stall for time. They decided to act very frightened.

Louise stuttered, "Wh-what will you do to us if we don't tell you where the guitar is?"

"I said you would be punished," the man repeated.

Jean had been backing away and heading toward her bunk. She had decided to try ringing the buzzer to summon the steward. With her hands behind her back, she finally found it and pushed hard and long.

Louise had been studying the intruder closely, now that her eyes had become accustomed to the dim light. She noticed that the shade of his hair was lighter than that of the man the girls had chased in the corridor. His face looked unnatural and she was convinced he was wearing a mask and a wig.

"Who are you?" she asked. "And what right have you to the guitar?"

"None of your sass," the man said belligerently. "You'd better tell me quick where that music box is!"

Jean countered with, "Suppose we don't know where it is?"

"You know all right," the man growled, taking a menacing step toward her.

It occurred to Louise that it might help if the girls screamed for help. As she opened her mouth to do so, the intruder put his hand into a pocket as if reaching for something. So he was not fooling! No doubt he had a concealed weapon with him and if necessary would use it.

To herself Jean was saying, "Oh, why doesn't the steward come?"

Louise, meanwhile, spoke to the intruder again. "You'll have to ask Captain Dana about the guitar."

"Don't give me any of that baloney," the man said angrily. "Well, do you tell me, or do I—"

At that moment there was a knock on the door.

"Come in!" Jean sang out.

The caller found the door locked. The girls' captor grinned maliciously in satisfaction. There was nothing the Danas could do, he knew. He stood between them and the door.

Louise cried out at the top of her voice, "I'm not going to tell you anything!"

"Oh, yes, you are!" the man exclaimed.

The shouting was so loud that it covered up the faint noise at the door. Someone was inserting a key and in a moment the door swung open. The steward stood there.

He stared in amazement at the scene before him. Quick as a wink the intruder turned, pushed the steward aside, and ran out.

"Grab him!" Jean cried out. "He threatened us!"

She and Louise ran into the corridor. By this time the steward had caught hold of the man and with the girls' help held him firmly. He struggled violently but was unable to get loose.

During the struggle, a male passenger walking down the corridor hurried toward them. At once Louise asked him if he would go into their cabin and telephone Captain Dana and Officer Matt Wilson.

"Please tell them to come here at once," she said. "We're the Dana girls."

The stranger willingly obliged, then asked if there was anything more he could do. "I see you're holding this man. Can I do it so you young ladies won't have to?" There was a faint smile on his face.

"Thank you," said Jean. "I admit we've had a big scare. This man locked us in our cabin and threatened us."

"I'm glad you caught him," the passenger said. "We shouldn't have people like that running around loose on the ship. Who is he?"

"We don't know," Louise replied. "But we'll soon find out."

Captain Dana and Detective Wilson arrived in a few minutes. Both were thunderstruck by what had happened.

"Who are you?" Captain Dana asked. "I don't remember seeing you on board."

The prisoner remained silent. Matt Wilson, turning to the girls, said, "Have you seen him before?"

Louise answered, "No, but I think he's wearing a mask and a wig."

Their prisoner, who by now had become tractable, was dragged to the cabin's porthole and the curtain pulled back. Quickly the detective stripped both a rubber face mask and a wig from the man.

"Now are you going to tell us who you are?" Wilson asked.

There was no need for the man to answer. Captain Dana recognized him at once. "He is one of the men who works in the galley—I think he's a pastry cook."

The prisoner did not deny this. Instead, he began to plead for mercy. "I didn't mean any harm. I wouldn't do anything bad to these girls."

"Then why were you here?" Captain Dana asked him sternly.

"I was bribed to get some information from them," the cook answered.

"What kind of information?" the skipper persisted.

"The man who bribed me only wanted to know where Gama Gomes's guitar is."

"I see," Matt Wilson spoke up. "Your name comes to me now. It's Renwick, isn't it?"

The cook nodded.

"Who is the person that bribed you?" Captain Dana asked.

Renwick hung his head. "I—I can't tell you."

"Why not?"

"He—he'd kill me," the man replied.

His listeners looked disgusted. Captain Dana said, "After you've been in the brig a while, maybe you'll feel more like talking."

The prisoner was led away.

After everyone had gone, Louise and Jean closed their door and flopped onto their bunks. "What a morning!" Louise said.

Jean frowned. "Do you realize that we still don't know who the briber is? Or who attacked Senhor Sarmento? And the identity of the cork thieves who are aboard?"

Louise admitted that things looked discouraging, but added, "I'm not giving up!"

"Oh, I'm not either," her sister said quickly. "I'm still very suspicious of Torres and Diogo. It's going to be hard shadowing them."

The girls changed to swimsuits and went at once to the open-air pool on A deck. They looked around for Torres and Diogo, but the men were not there. They did see Alfredo Moreira, the young man who had been Isabel's partner at the dance. He had been with Torres and Diogo.

The Danas stopped to speak to him and asked if he could tell them more about his two companions. Alfredo said the two men were not friends of his. He had met them for the first time the night of the dance. They had suggested he join them at the girls' table.

"I didn't like them and I haven't been with them since," Alfredo said.

He insisted that he knew nothing about the two and added, "They seemed very crude and brazen to me. I decided not to have anything more to do with them."

"Did you get an idea they're gypsies?" Louise asked him.

"No, I can't say I did."

Isabel appeared just then with two young men, and introduced them to Louise and Jean as Don and Judd.

"I decided not to swim until after lunch," Isabel said. "I promised to run back and see my father, but I'll return in time for lunch."

Don and Judd were very personable young men and the Danas had a lot of fun with them in the pool. By noon Isabel had returned. Alfredo joined them, and the three couples enjoyed a delightful luncheon together.

About an hour after they had finished eating, Louise suddenly said to Jean, "Here come Torres and Diogo. They have on their swim trunks."

As the two men walked past them, they paused and grinned at the girls.

"Hello," said Torres. "How about a date?"

"We're busy," Louise retorted.

Diogo laughed. "Don't think you can brush us off that easy. We'll be seeing you."

The girls' dates looked a bit annoyed and Louise and Jean hastened to assure them that they had no intention of being friendly with the two men.

At that moment Torres came back and said to Louise, "If we can't make a date with you now, how about Lisbon? Where will you be staying?"

"Can't tell you," Louise answered.

Torres left and presently he and his companion went into the pool. The girls watched the men swim around, then suddenly Jean had an impish idea. She whispered to Louise:

"Let's have a friendly water fight with Torres and Diogo and get samples of their hair!"

CHAPTER IX

Suspect Trapped

EXCUSING themselves to their escorts, Louise and Jean stood up.

"You don't mind, do you," said Louise, "if we give those men a ducking?"

"They deserve it," Don answered, laughing. "Want me to do it for you?"

"Oh, no, thanks," she answered quickly. "I'll see you in a few minutes."

Jean grinned. "Watch the fun."

The sisters hurried to the pool and gracefully dived in.

Surfacing, Jean whispered to Louise. "You take Torres. I'll get some of Diogo's hair."

"Right-o!" Louise giggled.

The two men were delighted by the girls' attention. But it soon became evident in the playful tactics which the Danas were using that they were far better swimmers than the men. After a little pretended wrestling, Torres and Diogo began to look frightened and make grabs for the ledge which ran around the four sides of the pool.

"We won't hurt you," Jean said gaily.

The onlookers were amused and one enthusiastic boy called out, "Duck 'em again! C'mon, duck 'em!"

"I dare you to pull 'em underwater!" another boy cried.

Everything was working out exactly as Louise and Jean had hoped. It was easy for them to duck the two men. During one of these playful moments, each of the girls grabbed her victim's hair and pulled out a few strands. The men did not seem to notice this as they tried to defend themselves and at the same time stay afloat.

As each girl accomplished her task, she swam to the edge of the pool and climbed out. Some of the young people, including Don and Judd, applauded the sisters. This embarrassed the men in the pool. They came out of the water immediately, pulled on their beach robes, and hurried away.

"Not even a good-by," Louise said with a mischievous grin.

She and Jean each had one fist closed over a few black hairs. Eager to take them at once to Detective Wilson, the girls made their apologies to their dates.

"We must go now," Jean said. "Work to do. It's been a grand day. Thanks a lot. We'll see you at the dance tonight."

When the sisters arrived at Officer Wilson's quarters, he was not there. A young man who was typing said he would try to locate the detective.

"I think he went down to the brig for a talk with Renwick to see if he could get any further information from him."

The young man made a phone call and presently the detective returned. He said he had had no luck with Renwick. He gazed at the girls in amusement. "You've been swimming," he said. "Something mighty important must have sent you here."

"We've brought clues you've been hoping for," Louise told him.

She and Jean opened their fists and showed the black hairs. The detective stared at them, then said, "Don't tell me these belong to Torres and Diogo!"

"Indeed they do," said Jean. "We had fun getting them. We plucked them out underwater and they didn't even yell."

"What do you mean?" the detective asked. When the girls told him the story, he laughed heartily and said, "Good for you! I'll bet those men's faces are red!"

"We don't expect that they'll ask us for a date again," Jean remarked, grinning.

Louise and Jean sat down while he went into his laboratory and put the hairs under his microscope. Presently he called out to the sisters to come in.

Looking up from the microscope, he said, "Diogo's hairs do not match the suspect's, but—"

"Yes?" Jean prodded him.

"These hairs of Torres's match those of the suspect's!"

"Hurrah!" Jean cried out. "We've solved the mystery!"

"It looks like it," the detective admitted. "I'll tell your uncle at once and have Torres brought here. And tell the barber not to bother any more about the hair clippings."

The Dana girls' hearts were pounding with excitement. How would Torres react to the interrogation? Would he really reveal why he had attacked Senhor Sarmento?

Fifteen minutes later Captain Dana walked in with the suspect. Uncle Ned locked the door so their prisoner could not escape. In concise and crisp tones Wilson confronted Torres with the evidence.

"Why did you attack Senhor Sarmento?" the detective asked him.

At once Torres became haughty. Angrily he said, "This is ridiculous! I know nothing of what you are talking about! I don't even know Senhor Sarmento!"

Captain Dana's face showed his annoyance. "Pretense will get you nowhere, Torres. Samples of your hair, pulled out by Senhor Sarmento during the struggle, were found in his cabin."

"That's crazy!" the man shouted.

Wilson did not pursue the subject. Instead, he

accused Torres of having bribed Renwick to force his way into the Dana girls' cabin and demand certain information.

"I don't know anything about that," the prisoner said.

"You lent him a face mask and a wig."

"That's a lie! I never owned a face mask or a wig."

There was silence for a few moments. The detective and the suspect both seemed to be trying to figure out what tack to take next. Before Wilson could speak up, Torres suddenly turned to Captain Dana and shouted:

"Why would I want to steal a guitar, anyway?"

Suddenly a grin crossed Captain Dana's face. "Who said anything about a guitar?" he asked. "Mr. Torres, I am afraid you have trapped yourself. Now you have two counts against you."

Torres, angry with himself, set his jaw firmly. He turned back to the detective with a sullen expression. "How did you get some of my hair to compare with the sample?"

It was Wilson's turn to smile. "That's our secret. Now suppose you tell us why you attacked Senhor Sarmento."

Torres smirked. "That's *my* secret. But I will tell you this. He deserved it!"

The prisoner announced that he was leaving now.

Captain Dana spoke up. "Oh, no, you're not.

"These hairs match those of the suspect's,"
the detective said

You're going with us to the brig. When we get to Lisbon, you'll be turned over to the authorities there. The penalty for a crime on the high seas is very severe."

Torres was taken away. The girls went back to their cabin to dress for dinner.

"That certainly was a worthwhile swim," Louise remarked. "We found out more in a short time than in all our previous sleuthing."

Before Jean had a chance to comment, their telephone rang. Detective Wilson was on the line. "Torres and Renwick deny knowing each other. By the way, I've decided to interrogate Diogo. Will you come to my office as soon as you can?"

"We'll be there in a flash," Jean answered.

The girls quickly finished dressing, locked their cabin, and hurried back to Matt Wilson's quarters.

Diogo refused to answer any questions. He insisted that he knew nothing of Torres's doings. "I met him one time in Portugal and again just before we booked passage in New York. The ship was crowded and he asked me if I would like to save money and share his cabin with him."

The detective ignored the remark, but said, "You're both gypsies, aren't you? Are you from the same tribe?"

"What do you mean?" Diogo retorted hotly. "I'm not a gypsy!"

Louise felt that nothing would be gained from

questioning the man further. An idea of a way to trap him popped into her mind. She sidled over to the desk and on a paper pad quickly drew the Romany symbol for sword. Picking it up, she casually slipped it in front of Diogo.

"That means cow, doesn't it?" she asked him, her question sounding innocent.

Without thinking, Diogo answered, "No, it means a sword."

The instant he had said this, Diogo regretted it. He realized that the remark had made him appear guilty.

Quickly Louise drew the other symbols which had been crayoned onto Gama Gomes's cabin. Again she held up the paper and said, "Together the symbols mean a warning of death."

Diogo was on guard this time. "I'm a Portuguese," he insisted. "Many people in Portugal know a few Romany words and have found out the meaning of some of the gypsy symbols. But it doesn't prove I'm a gypsy."

The girls, as well as Captain Dana and Detective Wilson, knew this was true. There was no excuse to hold Diogo and he was told he might leave. The man stalked off defiantly without another word.

Before Captain Dana went back to his duties, he said to his nieces, "You girls have been doing a great detective job. But you have only one full day remaining aboard the *Balaska* and I want you both to have some fun. Swim, play badminton, attend one of the lectures or art courses offered the passengers, and relax."

The sisters needed no further urging. After a late evening of dancing with Don and Judd, they were glad to pass the next morning basking in the sun by the pool. Since no further clues had turned up, Louise, Jean, and Isabel invited the boys to join them that afternoon for Ping-pong and shuffleboard.

As the girls were returning to their cabin to dress for dinner, they saw their uncle hurrying down the corridor.

"It looks as if you have been following my advice," he greeted them, smiling.

The girls happily related their activities of the day, then told him they were looking forward to the captain's gala dinner that evening.

"Which reminds me," he said, "Gama Gomes wants to entertain the guests tonight. He has begged to be allowed to play and sing for them. I believe it will be safe now that we are near the end of our journey, and have given him permission."

Dinner proved to be a gala affair indeed. Most of the guests were in evening clothes and had been given fancy paper hats to wear. Horns, whistles, and other noisemakers had been provided. The passengers lingered over the delicious meal and there was continuous music by the band and Gama Gomes. The minstrel received thunderous applause and finally he was called upon to talk to his audience.

"Speech! Speech!" they clamored.

His face flushed with embarrassment, the young musician stood up. "Thank you all very, very much. I hardly deserve the credit," he said, tapping his beautiful guitar. "All the credit goes to this instrument. It is a magic guitar."

"Magic!" one of his enthusiastic listeners called out.

The minstrel smiled but did not explain further. He thanked everyone again, hoped they would have a wonderful time in Portugal, and sat down.

One of the highlights of the evening was the fact that it had been considered safe for Senhor Sarmento to come to the dinner. He sat at the captain's table with his daughter, the Danas, and their dates. He thoroughly enjoyed himself. He was delighted by the news that his assailant had been found, but was completely at a loss to understand why he had been attacked. Senhor Sarmento felt that it had something to do with the theft of cork, but could not explain the connection, particularly if the man were a gypsy.

"If he personally had stolen a small quantity, that would be explainable," the manufacturer said. "But the thefts have been large—more than one gypsy could handle."

Everyone hoped that the mystery would be solved by the authorities in Lisbon. When the girls reached their cabin, Louise, Jean, and Isabel immediately got out their suitcases and started packing. The ship would dock about eight o'clock the next morning.

The three slept soundly but awoke early. They could hear signs of hustle and bustle aboard the *Balaska*. The girls had just finished dressing when the telephone rang. Louise picked up the receiver.

"Miss Dana?" said a man's worried voice.

"Yes—I'm Louise."

"This is Gama Gomes. Oh, Louise, my guitar has been stolen!"

CHAPTER X

The Escape

"How dreadful!" Isabel exclaimed when Louise related the minstrel's message. "You girls had better go down to talk to Gama and see if you can help him. I'll attend to our baggage."

"Thanks," Louise said.

She and Jean grabbed up their coats and purses, left generous gratuities for the steward, and hurried off. They found the minstrel greatly upset.

"I shall die if I do not get my guitar back!" he exclaimed, a catch in his voice.

"Please tell us what happened," Jean begged. "When did you first notice that the guitar was gone?"

"Just a few minutes ago," he answered. "We fellows got out of bed at the same time and dressed. The others started to leave, one by one, taking their own luggage and instruments with them. When I went to get my guitar from beneath the blanket it was gone! Vanished!"

The Danas asked Gama where he had kept the instrument and he pointed to his bunk. "I slept with it right alongside me. Someone must have unlocked the door, slipped in here, and taken it away from me."

The girls were heartsick over the matter, but hoped the instrument would be detected on someone trying to sneak it ashore.

"We'll find Uncle Ned at once," Louise said, "and ask him to have all the passengers searched before they leave the ship."

"Thank you," said Gama. "I'm too upset to ask him myself."

Louise and Jean hurried away to find their uncle. They finally caught sight of him on the bridge and told him what had happened.

"I can't understand it," he said, a puzzled expression on his face. "How did anyone get into the musicians' cabin without awaking the men?"

"Don't forget," Louise spoke up, "we found a skeleton key in your quarters and the cook Renwick managed to get into our cabin."

"That's right," Uncle Ned conceded. "I'll give orders at once that every person and every bit of baggage is to be checked carefully. We should be able to retrieve the guitar without too much trouble."

Louise and Jean hurried back to assure Senhor

Gomes of Captain Dana's help. Gama then asked hopefully, "Do you suspect anyone?"

Jean answered promptly, "Yes. I suspect Diogo. Louise, let's try to find him and watch him carefully when he carries his luggage off the ship."

Many people were milling about the decks, watching the *Balaska* dock at Lisbon. Everyone was intrigued by the great number of vessels, large and small, passenger and commercial, that lined the harbor.

"We'd better hurry," Louise advised.

She and Jean threaded their way among the passengers. Suddenly, on the aft deck where the hatch over the cargo hold was located, they saw Diogo. He was leaning on the rail and was looking out over the harbor as the *Balaska* steamed slowly to the pier. The cover of the cargo hold was open.

The girls walked toward Diogo, whose eyes were riveted on a motor launch which apparently had just pulled away from the *Balaska*. He did not notice Louise and Jean as they came up and stood near him.

Their eyes too followed the motor launch. On its side was painted *Rio Rosa*. Two men were in it, one in a crewman's uniform. The girls immediately focused on a large sack the other was holding on his knees.

Louise nudged Jean. "The stolen guitar could be in that sack!"

Her sister nodded and said, "Let's ask some

of the passengers if they saw it transferred from the *Balaska*."

The Danas separated and began to query several men standing around. Most of them had not seen anything, but one man answered Jean's question in the affirmative.

"Yes, I saw a sack being lifted out of the hold by one of the workmen around here. He climbed down the ladder on the side of the *Balaska* and then quickly jumped into the motor launch."

"A crewman?"

"Yes. Come to think of it, he did not carry the sack down with him. He tied a rope around it and lowered the sack to a man in the boat, then hurried down the ladder."

The stranger looked curiously at Jean. "Is something the matter?"

"Possibly. Would you say the sack was large enough to hold a guitar?"

"Yes. And its shape did look something like a guitar."

When Jean reported this conversation to Louise, her sister said, "Well, this exonerates Diogo. But who could that thieving crewman have been?"

The girls knew there was nothing more they could do. They decided to report the incident to Uncle Ned at once and ask him if he had given any crewman permission to leave the *Balaska* before the ship docked.

Captain Dana said he had given no such permission and was afraid the crewman had stolen the guitar and escaped. But everyone wondered how he had communicated with the motor launch.

"I think it was all prearranged," Louise said, and the others agreed.

The telephone near Uncle Ned rang. He answered it, listened for a moment, then shouted, "What!"

He motioned his nieces to come and hear the conversation. Jean and Louise put their ears to the telephone.

The crewman, who had charge of the ship's prisoners, was shouting, "That gypsy prisoner got out of his cell! He was locked up last night all right, but when I came just now to give him his breakfast he wasn't here!"

Captain Dana was angry and began to blame the crewman for being careless. Louise whispered to her uncle, "Probably Torres used a skeleton key."

At this, the captain calmed down a bit. He asked, "What about Renwick? Is he still in his cell?"

"Still here," the keeper replied, then continued, "Said he didn't see or hear anything next door to him. Must've slept through the whole confounded thing."

The Dana girls had a theory. It was just possible Garcia Torres had been let out of his prison by Diogo—then stolen a crewman's uniform, sneaked up to the musicians' quarters, and taken the guitar.

"He put it in the sack and went into the hold.

When the hatch cover was lifted, he climbed out."

Louise added gloomily, "And escaped."

After Captain Dana had hung up the telephone, he remarked that Torres was one of the slickest crooks he had ever come across. "I only hope he can be caught. No telling what a man like that will do next."

When the girls asked about their star witness Renwick, Captain Dana said, "I'm going to turn him over to the Lisbon police. Maybe they can get him to talk." Uncle Ned assured his nieces he would be in touch with them as soon as he had any news.

At the dock the Sarmentos, Louise, and Jean were met by Isabel's relatives, Senhor and Senhora Vasco, a handsome couple and very hospitable. Isabel called her father's sister *Tia* Maria and her husband *Tio* Ferdinand. They drove up the famous Avenide de Libertad, which was actually two streets with a wide tree-and-flower section in the center, lined with benches and mosaic sidewalks.

"What a beautiful avenue!" Louise remarked, gazing at the fine large hotels, offices, and apartments.

Aunt Maria said with a delightful accent, "We are very proud of our city."

Jean was drinking in the beautiful sunshine. "I know I'm going to love it here."

Uncle Ferdinand smiled. "That is good to hear. I hope you Dana girls will not be so busy with your detective work that you cannot enjoy yourselves."

Jean laughed. "I'll see to that."

The Vasco home was a beautiful Moorish-type house, set back a short distance from the street. There was a driveway which led to a walled-in garden at the rear. They turned in and a houseman opened a high iron gate to the grounds at the back. The large garden was splashed with colorful flowers, many of them camellias, and contained three large olive trees.

As Senhor Vasco opened the door to the house, his wife smiled and said, "*Está em sua casa.*"

Isabel translated. "It means, 'You are in your home.' This is what we Portuguese say to welcome you and make you feel at home."

"How lovely!" said Louise.

"Thank you."

The Danas were intrigued by the fine old hand-carved furniture and lovely damask draperies. As Senhora Vasco led the Danas to their room on the second floor, she pointed to a small door.

"There is a stairway behind that door leading to our lookout tower. It was an old Moorish custom to have such a tower," she remarked.

"Sounds mysterious," Jean remarked.

Several hours later Captain Dana telephoned the house to see that his nieces had arrived safely and to say good-by before sailing. He reported Renwick's transfer to the local police station and said he had been in touch with the harbor police also.

"I haven't very good news for you," he warned. "The *Rio Rosa* was found abandoned. It had been stolen, so there was no way to trace either the crewman or his passenger.

"Even if you girls locate the guitar," Uncle Ned went on, "you would not be able to return it to Gama. He wrote me a thank-you note, but left the ship without saying good-by or telling me where I could find him in Portugal."

"That's too bad," Jean said, "but maybe he'll get in touch with you. The poor minstrel was so upset he probably forgot everything."

The Sarmentos, Vascos, and the Dana girls felt discouraged over the whole affair. Jean and Louise proceeded to give Isabel's relatives a detailed account of all the happenings aboard ship during the trip from New York.

"You see, there's still a great deal for us to do," Louise told them.

"I wish you much luck," said Senhor Vasco.

"I guess we'll need it," Jean put in.

That night, when the girls went to bed, Louise found herself restless and unable to get to sleep. Finally she got up and looked out the window. What a beautiful moonlight night it was!

"I'll bet there's a marvelous view of the city from the tower," she told herself. "I think I'll go up there and take a look."

She put on a robe and slippers and went out to the hall. She unlocked the door to the tower and ascended the steps which showed up faintly between a low night light in the hall and moonbeams filtering in from above. She reached the top of the stairway and had just begun to gaze through one of the tower openings when something slapped her face hard. The blow nearly knocked her over. She screamed.

CHAPTER XI

Disaster Ahead

"Stop! Stop!" Louise cried out.

In the darkness she had no defense against the mysterious thing clawing at her face. She could hear the flutter of wings. Long, sharp talons scratched her cheeks.

"It's a bird!" she told herself. "I'd better get out of here fast!"

She descended the steps to the bedroom floor. Facing her were Jean and Isabel.

"Goodness! What ever happened to you, Louise?" Jean exclaimed. "We heard you scream in the tower. Did someone—?"

"Your face—it's all scratched and bleeding!" Isabel cried out.

Louise glanced at herself in a wall mirror and was horrified at her injuries. Both arms and hands were clawed as well as her face.

Isabel put an arm around her friend. "I'm terribly sorry," she said. "It must have been the big white stork that roosts in the tower at night."

Louise smiled ruefully. "I wish I had known he was there." She explained that unable to sleep, she had climbed up to the tower in order to get a view of the city at night. "But I had no chance!"

"We must attend to these scratches at once," Isabel said. "Come with me."

At that moment her aunt appeared, saying she had heard voices. Was something the matter?

Then, seeing Louise, she gasped in surprise and expressed her regrets. The Vascos had never tried to chase the white stork from the tower because of an old superstition that the bird was an omen of good luck.

"It was my own fault," Louise insisted. "I must wash my face and arms with cold water."

"Then we must apply an antiseptic to prevent infection," Senhora Vasco added.

The lotion she produced proved to be a bit of magic. By morning Louise's scratches were less painful, and barely noticeable after she covered them with face powder. She laughed, however, and said, "Nobody'll get me up in that tower again at night!"

At breakfast Senhor Sarmento announced he was ready to start his investigation of the cork thefts. "Are you detectives ready?" When they nodded, he said, "We may as well begin at the beginning."

Isabel asked him what he meant. "We'll drive directly to the cork oak forests and see what we can find out. We may get a clue to the thieves from one of the farmers."

The Danas learned that the Vascos were lending Senhor Sarmento their sedan, but were not going to join the group. Ready to leave, the visitors went out through the rear garden to the driveway where the car was parked. At that moment the side gate bell rang. Isabel went to answer it. Through the bars the Danas could see a pretty gypsy woman standing there, a basket over one arm.

"Just a minute," the girls heard Isabel say. She came back to speak to her father and the Vascos. "The gypsy is selling attractive copper bracelets. Shall I let her in?"

"We should leave at once," her father replied.

Louise and Jean looked at each other. They did not want to appear rude to their host, but hoped that the gypsy woman might be able to give them a clue to the whereabouts of Gama—or even perhaps of Torres and Diogo. The girls did not want to miss the opportunity of picking up one.

Louise spoke up quickly. "Senhor Sarmento, would it delay you too much to let us talk to the gypsy? I think we might learn something valuable about the stolen guitar and the hiding place of the two missing men."

He looked surprised but agreed. "Isabel, show her in, please."

The gypsy was young. Her large brown eyes scrutinized her audience in the garden, then roamed around looking at the trees, bushes, and flowers. She began to speak in Portuguese and Isabel translated for the Danas.

"You have a very beautiful home here," the gypsy said, smiling. "I hope you will like my bracelets."

"Did you make them?" Isabel asked her.

"No, the men of my tribe. They are excellent workers in copper."

"Isabel, ask her which tribe she belongs to," Louise requested.

Isabel put the question to the woman, who answered without hesitation, "The Ruk tribe."

The three girls were astonished. On shipboard Torres and Diogo had said when Gomes had not arrived that this would spoil all their Ruk plans. The girls' suspicions had been correct! The two men were gypsies and belonged to a tribe called the Ruks.

Jean asked Isabel to query the woman about the location of the tribe. This time her answer was evasive. With a smile she said, "We gypsies stay no place very long. We are always wandering about the countryside."

After each of the girls had purchased a bracelet, the woman offered to tell their fortunes. Since they had been good customers, she would not charge them anything extra.

Louise and Jean very much wanted to detain the gypsy and see what else they could find out from her. They pretended to be enticed by the idea of having their fortunes told.

"Please, Senhor Sarmento," said Jean, "let her read our palms."

Realizing that the girls would not have delayed him without a good reason, he consented. First the gypsy picked up Louise's hand, turned it over, and immediately frowned.

"You are from far across the big waters," she said. "But you never should have come away from home."

"Why not?" Louise asked.

"I see a young man you left behind. He is very unhappy and the sooner you get back to him the better."

Louise smiled. Before she had left the United States, her friend Ken Scott had teased her about the proposed voyage and her long absence. "Oh well," Louise thought, "it wouldn't take a gypsy fortuneteller with powers of clairvoyance to guess such a thing."

The woman went on to say that Jean was her sister, that the two girls were orphans and lived with an aunt and uncle. Louise thought, "This woman has certainly found out a lot about me. I wonder how. From Torres or Diogo or perhaps Gama?"

After telling Louise several other true facts, the

gypsy turned to Jean. Again she made such accurate statements that the girls were positive the woman had received the information from someone.

When she finished telling Jean's fortune, Louise said to her, "You are amazing. I suppose this is an art handed down from mother to daughter in your tribe."

"Yes, it is."

"And the men make copper articles and produce the music?"

"Yes."

"What do they play? I mean, what kind of instruments? Violas, violins, and guitars?"

"Yes."

"Did you ever hear of a fine guitar player named Gama Gomes?" Louise asked.

If she had hoped to take the woman off guard, Louise was disappointed. "No, I never heard of him," she answered.

Quickly the woman offered to tell Isabel's fortune. When she finished, the gypsy turned to Senhor Sarmento.

"I do not need to see your palm, the stars tell me that you are going on a very dangerous mission. You will subject your friends to it. Do not go. Great harm will come to all of you."

Senhor Sarmento laughed. "I know you gypsies," he said. "You are always telling people harm is going to come to them." He pulled a bill from his pocket and handed it to the woman. "Thank you and good-by."

The gypsy woman took the money but did not move. "You are making a grave mistake, sir. I have powers that see into the future. Yours is very bad unless you remain at your home."

He smiled. "I will take that chance."

As the girls escorted the woman to the gate, Jean whispered to Isabel to ask her how Torres and Diogo were. But when Isabel questioned the woman about the two men, she denied knowing them.

On the drive to Alentejo, the Danas told Senhor Sarmento their suspicions regarding the fortune-teller. "She certainly knew a great deal about us. I wonder if we were followed from the dock to the Vascos' home."

"Perhaps we are being constantly watched," Louise remarked. "Could we ask the authorities to locate the Ruk tribe?"

"Yes, indeed. I will do it as soon as we return from our trip."

Some time later they reached the balmy area of Alentejo, and passed grove after grove of cork oaks.

"It is too early in the season to strip them," said Senhor Sarmento. "But when we get to a certain farm, I'll ask the man, whom I buy from, to give us a demonstration."

Presently he pulled off the road and drove up to a whitewashed cottage. An attractive flower garden surrounded it and everything about the place was spick-and-span.

The door was opened by a short, smiling, dark-haired man who wore a small mustache.

"Senhor Sarmento!" he exclaimed. "What a joyful surprise! Come right in."

The cork products manufacturer introduced his daughter and the Dana girls. Senhor Sebastian's plump, smiling wife came from the kitchen and made the group welcome. The Danas were intrigued by the simple furnishings and a tall chimney which occupied the center of the house. Many copper articles, including carefully scoured pots and pans, gleamed from their hooks on the walls.

Senhora Sebastian insisted the visitors have luncheon with them. She said they were having *porco à alentejana.* Isabel told them this meant pieces of pork stewed with clams. The combination of pork and clams did not appeal to Louise and Jean, but they managed to smile pleasantly. To their amazement, the dish was very tasty and they had second helpings, together with bread and cheese and home-bottled grape juice.

During the meal the two men discussed the business which had brought them together. Senhor Sebastian was alarmed to hear about the shortages in the cork products arriving in the United States.

Furthermore, by comparing notes, the men discovered that shipments of raw cork scheduled to arrive at the Lisbon plant were far overdue.

"Every load which goes out of here I count personally and I know my men are honest," the farmer said.

"It's certain," said Senhor Sarmento, "that someone, somewhere, is stealing part of the raw product, and later holding back some of the shipment of finished products to the United States. Have you any idea who or where this might be?"

Senhor Sebastian thought for some time, then finally he said, "Perhaps I can offer one clue."

CHAPTER XII

Mad Donkey

EVERYONE waited anxiously to hear what Senhor Sebastian was going to tell them about the cork thefts. He leaned forward across the table and said:

"Perhaps it is gypsies. One day when we were working in the cork forest, stripping trees and packing the bark onto our carts, a tribe of gypsies rode through. Later we noticed that an entire wagonload was missing."

"Do you know what tribe they were from?" Jean spoke up.

"No, I do not."

Senhor Sarmento told the farmer he had promised to show the girls how the cork trees were stripped. Senhor Sebastian smiled. "I shall be glad to."

He led the way from the little house. First he showed them the great wooden wagon with the solid wooden wheels in which the cork strippings were carried. "There is always a team of oxen to draw each cart to the processing plant," he explained to the girls.

Senhor Sebastian said that at the plants the cork strippings were put through a hot purifying bath to rid the bark of any insects or other foreign matter. Next, the bark was carried to the factory where the inner and outer sections were separated.

"Sometimes the inner brownish-colored part is used for making various products like table mats. More often, however, it is ground up with the outer bark and the particles compressed with a glue-like filler.

"Now I think we're ready to go to one of the cork groves," Senhor Sebastian suggested.

The Danas marveled at the size of the cork trees. Some were as tall as any of the oak trees they had seen in the United States. The farmer had brought tools and now summoned a man who was working nearby to help him strip a tree.

"This cork oak is about a hundred and fifty years old," he said. "That is about the life span for stripping. We do not start work on the trees until June, and then we work through August or September."

"How often can you strip the trees?" Louise asked.

"Once every ten years. It takes about that long for a new covering to grow. We don't like to cut it off until it's four to six inches thick."

The girls watched intently as the two farmers made two long vertical cuts about four feet apart. Next, they made a horizontal cut near the bottom of the tree. Finally the workmen climbed up a stepladder and made another horizontal cut about ten feet higher up.

Now they were ready to strip the tree. Deftly the two men began to yank off the section which had been cut out. The long strip was laid on the ground. Senhor Sarmento said, "These trees are quite a phenomenon. That pinkish bark you see on that tree is the real bark. That is why stripping does not kill the tree."

Jean and Louise looked somewhat puzzled. Louise spoke up. "I thought what these men stripped off was the bark."

"No," Senhor Sarmento said. "Not the real bark. What has been taken off for commercial use is merely a protective cover to help the tree retain moisture in long periods of very dry, hot weather."

Jean asked when man first discovered the use of cork. Senhor Sebastian laughed. "We have no idea. In the year 400 B.C. it was already in use."

From his pocket he took a magnifying glass. "I want you to look closely at the inside of the section we just cut off. You'll notice a very perfect and unusual formation. The cork is a mass of air cells that never touch each other. Look at the pith around them. That's what makes cork so buoyant."

Senhor Sarmento added, "And no matter how

tightly you compress cork, it will still float. It is used for hundreds of things, including bottle stoppers, life preservers, floats, and buoys. The Navy fits cylindrical pieces of cork into their great guns. The cork inserts take up the shock and keep the firing mechanism from becoming dented."

He had just finished speaking when one of the workmen cried out to them excitedly in Portuguese. Quickly Isabel translated. "Look out! Run!"

The Danas turned to see a frisky donkey galloping in their direction. Suddenly he reared straight up and began to snort strangely.

The three girls and the men took refuge behind trees. In seconds the braying animal was chasing one of the workmen around a tree and trying its best to kick him.

"He'll kill us!" Louise thought.

There was wild confusion as the mad donkey raced from person to person, forcing each one to seek a new hiding place. The siege lasted for ten minutes, then suddenly the animal collapsed to the ground, its eyes bulging and froth oozing from its mouth.

"The poor thing!" Louise remarked. "He must be ill."

"I think he has been poisoned," Senhor Sebastian said.

Jean asked if it could have eaten a form of lo-

"Look out! Run!" Isabel cried excitedly

coweed. "We have that in our country and it drives livestock mad."

The farmer shook his head. "No, we do not have such a weed here." He went over to look at the donkey.

"Is he going to die?" Isabel asked, pity in her voice.

"I do not know. If he continues to be in great pain, I will have to shoot him. But that would sadden my wife. This donkey is a great pet of hers."

Isabel said she did not want to watch the poor animal suffer, nor be there if he had to be shot. "Let's go back to the Sebastian home now," she suggested to the other girls, who were glad to leave also.

Senhor Sarmento joined them. On the way they discussed who would have been so heartless as to poison the pet donkey.

"I think it is a form of revenge," Isabel's father replied.

"Revenge?" Jean repeated. "Revenge for what?" Senhor Sarmento said he believed it was somehow tied in with the theft of the cork. "I am sure it was a *hokkane baco*."

"What's that?" Louise asked.

"A gypsy trick."

He went on to say that they had better leave now. "I want to visit another farm that supplies me with cork."

He told Senhora Sebastian he would telephone her husband very soon. The visitors thanked the woman for her hospitality and drove off.

The next farmer they visited was named Campani. He reported he had not missed any cork from his place. However, the receiving agents at Senhor Sarmento's plant had reported shortages to Campani's drivers.

"I am sure all my men are honest. It is my personal opinion that part of the loads were stolen from my delivery wagons while en route."

"And you have no idea how?"

Senhor Campani said he did not, but would call in a couple of his men for questioning. When the workmen arrived, the actual questioning was turned over to the Dana girls. Isabel's father explained to Senhor Campani that the sisters had solved many mysteries and were helping to solve this one.

"Please go ahead, girls," he said.

Louise smiled. "When you were transporting a load of cork, did you ever stop along the way?" she asked the men.

With Isabel and her father translating the Danas' questions and the men's answers, the conversation proceeded. The men admitted they frequently stopped along the road for fairly long periods.

"To eat and to rest the animals," one of them added.

"Were there any other people around?" Jean put in.

The workmen looked a little sheepish as they answered, "Several members of a gypsy tribe happened to be passing each time when we made a stop."

Louise and Jean looked at each other. Here was a clue!

"Did you talk with the gypsies?" Louise queried.

Again the answer was in the affirmative. "Some of the gypsies offered to share their food with us," one man said, "and invited us to play wrestling games with them in the fields. One of their men was a fortuneteller. We paid him to tell us about our future."

Louise and Jean were sure now Senhor Campani's suspicions were correct. No doubt during this game period other gypsies had removed many strips of cork from the wagon and put them into their own wagons. The loot was well covered with tarpaulin so Campani's men were not suspicious of the thefts.

Senhor Sarmento asked the workmen, "How many times did you stop and talk to gypsies?"

The men thought about this, then one of them replied, "About six."

"Were any names mentioned?" Jean queried.

"Yes. Two of them were called Fero and Yerko."

"Did you notice anything to identify what tribe they belonged to?" Louise asked.

The workman nodded. "I seem to remember that some of the gypsies had the figure of a tree tattooed on their foreheads."

Louise and Jean looked at each other, excited over the information. The gypsies must be members of the Ruk tribe!

CHAPTER XIII

Sabotage

BEFORE the Danas left the farm, Senhor Campani warned them that tracking down the Ruks would not be easy.

"Gypsies move quickly and if they think they are being sought by the police or detectives, they will go in hiding. They can be dangerous, too, when they become angry. If you do find them, you'd better take along a policeman."

The girls thanked him for his good advice and started the return trip to Lisbon with the Sarmentos. Most of the conversation was about the clues they had picked up that day.

"It was a very worthwhile trip," Senhor Sarmento commented. He laughed lightly. "You Danas remind me of an old Latin saying, 'To swim without cork.' It means 'needing no assistance.' "

"How quaint!" Louise commented.

Jean remarked, "It looks as if we'll need plenty of cork to keep our heads above water in this case."

Senhor Sarmento was quiet for some time, then spoke up suddenly. "I have been thinking about you girls continuing to work on this mystery. There have been certain elements of danger, and I feel that things are going to get worse. This is really a man's job and I think I had better hire a detective to investigate the cork thefts."

The girls' spirits fell. Just when they were hot on the thieves' trail, they were being asked not to go any farther! They became silent and after a while Isabel's father realized he had dampened their ardor.

To make up for this, he said cheerfully, "Girls, I do not want you to feel too bad about my decision. You have my permission to do some safe sleuthing."

Jean looked puzzled. "What is safe sleuthing?"

Senhor Sarmento thought about this a moment. "How about trying again to find the guitar?"

"But the gypsies probably have it," Louise reminded him.

"That is true," he agreed. "Well, it is possible you may pick up a clue right in Lisbon. In any case, I think that tomorrow you should enjoy some sightseeing."

"We're eager to see your beautiful city," Louise said politely, trying to cover up her hurt feelings.

As soon as they reached home, the girls eagerly asked the Vascos if they had any news for them.

Isabel's lovely aunt smiled. "You girls have a big fat letter from home. Isn't that good news?"

"Indeed it is!" Jean answered. "But have you heard any more from Uncle Ned about Gama or the missing guitar?"

The woman shook her head. "Unfortunately no."

Senhor Sarmento immediately telephoned police headquarters. When he learned there had been no word of Gama Gomes and that Renwick was being uncooperative, Isabel's father told what he had learned about the Ruks.

"We are sure the tribe is mixed up in the cork thefts and the missing guitar," he said confidently, and added, "We are also certain two gypsies called Garcia Torres and Sylvestre Diogo are members of the tribe. These men are our chief suspects. We also think two others named Fero and Yerko are cork thieves."

The police chief agreed it was a good lead and would alert his men. "They will go out at once to start the hunt."

When Senhor Sarmento finished his conversation, Louise suggested Gama might be a prisoner of his own tribe!

"More likely he's hunting for the magic guitar," Jean added. "I certainly hope we hear something soon."

When the Danas came into the dining room the following morning, Senhor Vasco greeted them with *"Bom dia."* The girls smiled and said, "Good morning to you, too."

Isabel was there and said excitedly, "Guess what? Senhor Sebastian's donkey is all right. They did not have to shoot it."

"That is good news," Louise said. "And it will be even better news when we learn who poisoned the poor thing."

Senhor Sarmento planned to go to his factory, so Senhora Vasco offered to take the girls sightseeing. She outlined their trip and asked them to be ready to leave in half an hour. They finished breakfast, then went upstairs to get sweaters.

A few minutes later the three girls and Senhora Vasco walked out to the garage. Suddenly all of them gave cries of dismay. The car was a mess.

"Sabotage!" Isabel exclaimed.

Tires had been slashed, the windshield splashed with paint, and all the upholstery torn.

"This is dreadful!" Louise said.

Senhora Vasco was speechless. She just kept mumbling, "Oh! Oh! Oh!"

Isabel put an arm around her aunt's waist. "I know this is upsetting," she said, "but we can all be glad nothing happened to any of us. After all, the car can be replaced."

Finally Senhora Vasco said, "How did the vandal get in here? The gate is always kept locked."

"I have a theory," Louise spoke up. "A gypsy who has a skeleton key."

"Torres or Diogo!" Jean exclaimed. She went on to say that the gypsy fortuneteller, who had been at the Vascos' the previous morning, might have reported the location of the garage.

Senhora Vasco was fearful. "If it's possible to get in here that easily, our enemy may come again and do more damage."

She opened the door on the driver's side, with the idea of getting in and seeing if the car would start. For the first time she noticed a note on the front seat.

"What's this?" the agitated woman cried out. Then, reading the message on it, she said in Portuguese, "*Nao viaja*. That means 'do not travel.'"

Although everyone was angry at the audacity of the saboteur, they were also determined to find out who he was. The Danas suggested that the police be notified at once. Within ten minutes two officers appeared. They took photographs, made many notes, then took samples of fingerprints on the car.

The Danas assumed their sightseeing trip had been canceled, but Senhora Vasco, regaining her composure, said that she would telephone for a rented car and they would make the trip. The Danas were about to say this was not at all necessary, when Isabel remarked, "That is a good idea, Tia

Maria. It will get your mind off this horrible event."

In a short time the rented car appeared at the house and the group started out on the sightseeing trip. Senhora Vasco seemed to be her calm self again. As she drove, Jean and Louise admired the colorful stucco houses of pink, blue, and pale green. When they reached the Tagus River, the girls were intrigued by the many sailboats on it. Some had heavy red sails and looked most picturesque.

When the visitors reached the imposing Jeronimos Church, the Danas were fascinated by it. "What a beautiful place! And so huge!" Jean cried out.

Senhora Vasco explained, "This monastery was built to illustrate in stone Portugal's great Age of Discovery."

When the girls entered and walked around, they realized what she meant. The great columns had stone fish entwined with vines, and red lamps glowed above carved African lions.

"The tombs of many of our queens and kings are here," Isabel explained.

The Danas noticed that the catafalques rested on the backs of marble elephants. Isabel pointed out the tomb of Vasco da Gama and said, "He was the first man to find a route to India."

"And here's the tomb of our beloved poet Camoes," Senhora Vasco said. "He not only wrote poems but went on voyages too. Once, he made a trip to the Orient, which in the days of sailing vessels was a daring and marvelous accomplishment."

When the sightseers came out of the church, Senhora Vasco drove back into the business section. On one street the girls noticed a crowd had gathered to watch a man doing sleight-of-hand tricks.

"Let's watch him!" Jean said.

Isabel's aunt stopped and the girls got out. Since she could not park close by, Senhora Vasco said she would drive around the corner and wait for them up the street.

As the three girls neared the magician's audience, they suddenly saw one man push into another, then back away. In his hand was a wallet which he quickly slipped into his pocket.

"Jean!" exclaimed Louise. "That's Torres!"

As the girls turned around to look for a policeman, the man whom Torres had pushed cried out in dismay, "My wallet is gone!"

By this time Torres had moved off. The girls ran after him. They looked left and right for a policeman but none was in sight.

A few seconds later the girls heard pounding footsteps behind them. They looked over their shoulders to see a man running pell-mell toward them. He was shouting something in Portuguese.

Isabel stopped and motioned to the girls to do the same.

"What is that man yelling?" Jean asked.

Isabel had turned pale. "He is calling, '*Pare! Pare! Pare!*' That means 'Stop!'"

The girl listened for a moment, then said, "He is telling us, 'The lady with you has been injured!'"

CHAPTER XIV

Prisoner's Plea

By now the Dana girls had given up hope of pursuing Torres. They were horrified to hear Senhora Vasco had been injured and hurried back up the street with Isabel.

The man who had given them the message had disappeared. "Did you recognize him, Isabel?" asked Louise.

"Yes, I got a good look at him. He was the magician."

The girls found Senhora Vasco seated in her car about two blocks up the street. To their astonishment, she was calmly reading a newspaper and listening to the car radio.

Isabel opened the door and exclaimed, "Tia Maria, you are all right?"

Senhora Vasco smiled. "Yes, dear. I'm all right. What made you think otherwise?"

While Isabel was explaining, Louise and Jean tried to figure out the reason for the hoax.

"We certainly were fooled," Louise spoke up.

"Another *hokkane baco*," Jean guessed.

After some further discussion, Senhora Vasco and the girls concluded the episode had been staged. The performer, who was no doubt a gypsy, had attracted the attention of a crowd. Then, when people were successfully distracted by his tricks, Torres had sneaked up and neatly slipped the leather wallet from the unsuspecting man's pocket.

"Our arrival spoiled Torres's plans," Jean said.

"You're probably right," Isabel agreed. "When the magician realized we might capture Torres, he thought up a clever way to stop us and it worked."

The Danas chided themselves for having been duped by the two men. The girls got into the car and in a few minutes their good humor returned. Louise remarked how glad she was Senhora Vasco was all right.

Jean, giggling, remarked, "Who knows? We may have saved a lot of people from having their purses or wallets stolen."

The Danas asked if they might take time to buy some gifts for special people at home.

"I'd like to take our Aunt Harriet one of those lovely hand-embroidered tablecloths and napkins," Louise said.

"And I want to buy a pair of lovely cork bookends for Mrs. Crandall, the headmistress of our school," Jean added.

After the purchases were made, Senhora Vasco

headed home. The damaged automobile had already been towed away, so she drove the rented car into the garage. It was such a delightfully sunny and warm day she suggested they have luncheon on the patio. A maid served them a delicious fruit salad.

While they were eating dessert, the maid came to tell them there was a small boy at the front door who wanted to talk to the Dana girls. Louise and Jean exchanged puzzled looks as they rose quickly from the table.

"Excuse us, please." The girls smiled at their hostess and followed the maid inside.

Louise opened the front door. A rather ragged urchin stood there. He was a handsome boy and had a nice smile.

"You Dana girls?" he asked in halting English, giving each sister a sweeping look.

"Yes. What can we do for you?" Louise inquired.

The boy brought a soiled piece of paper from his pocket. It had been folded over several times. "Man say bring paper to you."

The boy handed the paper to Louise, then turned quickly and ran off down the street.

"That was a funny one," Jean remarked with a puzzled frown. "But let's unfold the paper and see what it is."

The message was signed Gama. It was scrawled in pencil and said:

I am prisoner Ruks. Will play Alfama
tonight. Move tomorrow Sintra.

As soon as Louise and Jean had read the note, they hurried back to join Isabel and her aunt and related the curious message.

"Sintra is a town west of here, isn't it?" Jean questioned.

Senhora Vasco nodded.

"Yes, it is about twenty miles from Lisbon," Isabel put in. "There's a shuttle train between the towns." She paused for a moment, then turned to Jean and Louise. "We could—"

"No, Isabel," Senhora Vasco interrupted, "I do not think it is safe for you to travel alone. I am sure your father will be very happy to drive you girls to Sintra."

"What is Alfama?" Louise asked.

She was told it was a very old section of Lisbon. The streets were narrow and there were many places of entertainment.

"Over there you will hear lots of music and see plenty of dancing," Senhora Vasco said.

"Oh, may we go there tonight?" Louise asked eagerly.

Senhora Vasco thought a moment, then said, "This may be another gypsy trick. Gama may not have written this note. Going to the Alfama might be a trap for you girls."

"It is odd the Ruks are letting their prisoner perform in Alfama," Louise admitted.

Jean agreed, but suggested the Ruks might have decided to take advantage of the minstrel's talent. "Gama will probably have to turn over any money he makes."

"I agree," Isabel spoke up. "Tia, wouldn't it be all right to go if you and Tio Ferdinand accompany us? After all, Jean and Louise should see and hear some of our native songs and dances."

Her aunt said she would consult her husband when he returned. Toward the end of the afternoon he came in, and after hearing about the note and the Danas' desire to do some sleuthing in the Alfama, he gave his consent.

"Oh, thank you," the girls said gratefully.

Senhor Vasco smiled. "Now don't get your hopes up too high. It may be hard to find Gama Gomes in the Alfama."

Jean and Louise said Senhora Vasco had told them of the maze of streets and numerous places of entertainment.

When Senhor Sarmento returned, he was amazed to learn of the day's happenings. Smiling, he said, "I think you girls are making good headway on the mystery."

At eight o'clock the six set off for the Alfama. They parked the car, then began walking. At several places the two men went inside, while the women waited near the front entrance. Senhores Sarmento and Vasco were having no luck finding the minstrel.

The searchers had walked several blocks when suddenly Louise called out, "Listen!"

Everyone came to a sudden halt as they too heard the plaintive sound of a man singing a sad ballad to the accompaniment of a guitar.

"I never heard that song before," Isabel remarked, then listened for a moment. "The singer's telling the story of a crime."

"He sounds just like Gama!" Jean exclaimed.

"It *must* be Gama!" Louise echoed.

The group hurried into the restaurant. By this time the performer had finished his song and left the room. The group was shown to a table. Before sitting down, Isabel said to the waiter, "Is Gama Gomes singing here tonight?"

"No, Senhorita," he replied, and briskly turned away.

"Shall we leave?" Isabel asked the others.

The Danas vigorously shook their heads. "I think we should wait until the singer returns for his next performance. Perhaps Gama is using an assumed name."

Senhor Sarmento said he thought this would be a fine opportunity to have dinner and see some of the folk dances.

Isabel leaned toward Jean and Louise. "I recommend you try *bife na frigadeira*. That is steak with a special mustard sauce. I'm sure you'll like it."

The Danas agreed to try it. But when it came,

they took one taste, then scraped most of the sauce from the meat. It was too hot for their taste!

Jean and Louise were fascinated by a group of colorfully dressed men and women from one of the provinces who performed an intricate dance. The Danas hoped they would have an opportunity to learn the attractive steps sometime. The number was followed by a woman completely dressed in black. She sang a melancholy song about a lost lover.

"Why doesn't she sing something cheerful?" Jean asked Isabel.

"The most popular song in Portugal is the *fado* and it is traditionally sad," was the answer.

The girls anxiously waited for the male singer to return. When the manager came to their table and asked if everything was satisfactory, Louise inquired about the guitarist.

"What is his name?"

"Muja," the manager answered.

"That's a gypsy name, isn't it?" Isabel queried. The manager nodded.

After he had walked off, the group discussed this latest bit of information. Had Torres been telling the truth when he said the minstrel's real name was not Gama Gomes? Was Gama's gypsy name Muja? Or had his captors given him an assumed name? Or perhaps the singer was someone else!

There was further entertainment but still Muja

did not appear. After a while the manager waved the band to stop playing and announced that Muja had been taken ill and been forced to leave.

"Oh no!" Jean cried out. "Now we've lost our chance to see him!"

Patrons around were amused by the girl's remark. They thought, of course, she must be a loyal fan of his. Jean got up quickly and rushed over to the manager.

"My friends and I must see Muja," she insisted. "Where is he?"

"I'm sorry, senhorita, he has left with friends."

"Please tell me what he looked like," Jean went on.

The man smiled and answered obligingly. "He's very dark, has black hair, and is quite handsome. But you might say the most distinctive thing about him is his magic guitar."

Jean was excited by this news. She was sure now that Muja was Gama Gomes and the stolen guitar was once more in his possession. She returned to the table and told the others.

While they were talking, the waiter brought the bill. He looked around furtively, then shoved a piece of paper into Louise's hand. Under his breath, he said, "Muja saw you girls from the doorway and asked me to give this to you."

Quickly Louise unfolded the paper. Three symbols had been drawn on a billhead of the restaurant.

Wide-eyed, the waiter was staring at the notations.

"Do you know what they mean?" Louise asked him.

"No. But I would say you had better be careful." He went off with money which Senhor Vasco had handed him for the bill.

Louise showed the symbols to the others in the group but none of them knew what they meant. Senhora Vasco said she had a book at home which described gypsy customs and contained a vocabulary of Romany symbols.

As soon as they reached the house, she brought it out and quickly the mysterious message was translated. The three symbols meant tree, moon, and house. This last one was double, with one house atop another.

"What in the world does it mean?" Isabel asked, then thought a moment. "Perhaps the tree symbols refer to members of the Ruk tribe."

"Maybe, but I have another guess," said Jean. "Muja is coming to this house and when the moon is up, he is going to climb a tree to our second floor."

"And then what?" Isabel queried. "Is he going to ask for asylum?"

Senhor Sarmento said with a smile, "I think not, but he may ask us to keep the guitar so it won't be stolen."

The Danas were skeptical that this was the

answer. Nevertheless they were curious to see if Jean's hunch about the message would be carried out. The moon had already started rising. It would not be long now.

Louise and Jean went to their second-floor bedroom which overlooked the garden with its three olive trees and waited eagerly.

CHAPTER XV

Mysterious Note

An hour went by and nothing happened. The moonlight was very bright. Outside, objects and their shadows were vivid.

"We may as well go downstairs again," Louise suggested.

They found the Vascos and Senhor Sarmento there with Isabel. All were confident the note was perhaps another *hokkane baco*. Louise and Jean did not agree but could offer no proof to the contrary.

Isabel served glasses of lemonade and the conversation turned to further sightseeing plans for the girls.

"May we go to Sintra soon?" Jean asked. "Gama Gomes may be there. Remember?"

Isabel's father said, "Yes. But even if you do not find Gama or the Ruk tribe, the place is certainly worth visiting."

"Indeed it is," Senhora Vasco put in.

She told the girls about the interesting old palace and the fantastic Peña Castle that stood on top of a wooded mountain. It had been added to from time to time and was a conglomeration of Moorish and various types of European architecture.

"And then there's Montserrate," she went on, "with its beautiful gardens. Botanists say there are ninety species of various plant life growing there that are not found anywhere else in the world."

"Sounds wonderful!" Louise exclaimed.

She was about to ask what it was like inside the castle when there was a loud, dull thud.

"What was that?" Senhora Vasco said, somewhat startled.

Everyone sprang from his chair and tried to trace the cause of the sound. Nothing in the house had fallen and two servants who were in the kitchen said they had no idea where the noise had originated.

"Let's check outside," Jean suggested, opening the back door.

They all hurried into the garden. Senhor Vasco went to make certain the gate was still locked. His wife and Isabel checked to see that nothing was amiss on the patio.

Meanwhile, Louise and Jean had walked toward the far end of the garden. Suddenly Jean put a hand on her sister's arm. "Did you hear a noise?"

Without waiting for a reply, Jean scurried over to a high group of bushes and plunged into their midst. In a few moments she returned, scratched and dirty. "False alarm," she admitted sheepishly to her sister.

As soon as the group went inside, Louise hurried to the front door and opened it wide.

"Oh!" she exclaimed.

"What is it?" Isabel asked, running forward with Jean.

The others gathered to see what Louise had discovered. She pointed to the outside of the door where a piece of paper had been speared by a long hunting knife!

Louise was about to reach for the knife when Senhor Vasco cried out, "Don't touch that! Leave it alone! There may be poison on the handle!" Louise gasped and chided herself for being so careless.

Isabel ran for a kitchen towel and handed it to her uncle. Carefully he wrapped the cloth around the handle of the knife, then pulled it out of the door. As he held it up, the group could see Romany-type symbols which had been drawn on the side of the paper against the door.

"How weird!" Louise remarked.

At once Isabel ran off to get the book on gypsy customs. The others continued to stare at the symbols.

After some research in the book, the girls translated the first symbol to mean, "children travelers," and the second, "men travelers." The third was one the Danas had seen before which meant a man's sword.

"It looks like another warning," Senhora Vasco said grimly. "Ferdinand, what do you think it means?"

Her husband had lowered his head and began to pace back and forth. "This is very bad, very bad! It is a warning for our guests to depart immediately, probably for home. They will be harmed unless they follow the instructions."

Isabel quivered at the threat. She sensed her father too was in great danger. Was it possible the suspected Ruks who were after Senhor Sarmento were now threatening the Danas as well?

"Perhaps we should go back to New York," Isabel said fearfully.

Her father stalked up and down the hall. Senhor Vasco closed the front door and laid the knife with the note on a table. In a moment his brother-in-law turned to him.

"I am not going to be scared off by these thieves!" he said with determination. "I will stay here until we get to the bottom of this mystery!"

Louise and Jean were thrilled. Now they could remain and help to solve both the mystery of the cork thefts and the minstrel's guitar. Gama, they felt sure, had been whisked away from the restaurant by the same men who were holding him prisoner. In this way they had spoiled his plan to escape and see the girls.

Senhor Sarmento seemed to be reading the Danas' thoughts. He told them exactly what was going through their minds. The girls smiled.

"We try to reason things out logically," Louise told him, "but sometimes we play hunches."

"And do they work?" he asked.

"Indeed they do."

Senhor Sarmento inquired what hunches the sisters had now. Jean was the first to answer. "Mine is that the mystery of the cork thefts and the minstrel's guitar will prove to be connected."

"My hunch," Louise added, "is that something is going to happen tonight that may solve these mysteries."

This remark worried Senhora Vasco. She said that perhaps they should call the police. Her husband put an arm around the woman's shoulders and assured her this would not be necessary.

"We are well protected here," he insisted.

Louise and Jean questioned this. Someone had used a skeleton key to get into the garden! He might use it again! The girls said nothing to the others, however.

The first floor of the house was locked securely and everyone went to his room. The Danas did not turn on their lamp because their room was bright with moonlight. They walked to the casement window, leaned their elbows on the sill, and looked outside.

"Isn't it romantic?" Louise said. "It doesn't seem

possible that in this lovely, peaceful scene any human being could be planning to harm another."

Her sister agreed and said, "It doesn't seem possible, either, that so many unpleasant things have happened since our arrival in Lisbon."

The girls became silent for fully a minute. Then suddenly Jean tugged on Louise's arm and pointed downward. A man was climbing the olive tree which grew just outside their window!

CHAPTER XVI

An Accident

As THE man climbed the olive tree, Louise and Jean drew back out of the path of the brilliant moonlight. They hid on either side of the window behind some draperies and watched the ascending figure. Who was he? Gama? Or an enemy?

When the man reached window level, he stopped and the girls got a good look at him. This person was a stranger with blond hair. He was definitely not Gama, Torres, or Diogo.

Who was he? Just a common thief, or was he somehow connected with the mysteries they were trying to solve?

"Maybe he's Fero or Yerko," they reasoned. "He might even be another member of the Ruk tribe."

Jean dropped to the floor and crawled over to Louise. In a whisper she said, "If he should come in, shall we nab him?"

"Yes."

The stranger made no attempt to come in. A few moments later he began to whistle softly as if to attract someone's attention. Warily the girls appeared at the window, but at such an angle that if the man should throw anything at them they would not be hit.

But he made no attempt to act in an unfriendly manner. Instead, he called out softly, "I must talk to you."

The girls showed their faces. Suddenly they recognized the caller.

"You're the accordionist in the band at the restaurant!" Jean exclaimed.

"Yes, I am Manuel," he said softly. "Please forgive this strange way of calling on you. The request came from your friend Gama Gomes."

"How did you get into the garden?" Louise asked him, but her voice was not harsh.

"He gave me a key to the gate. Said it was all right for me to come in. He asked me to do just what he intended to do, but he did not explain why. I hope I have not committed any crime by coming in."

The girls did not comment on this. Jean asked him to tell them more about Gama Gomes.

"His gypsy name is Muja," the man told them. "He said he is in great trouble and needs help. You are the Dana girls from America?"

"Yes."

"Gama did not tell me what trouble he is in, but said you are his only friends in Portugal and would help him."

Louise spoke up. "We expected to see him ourselves tonight."

The accordionist said that Gama had planned to come and call on the girls. "But he was taken ill and could not play. Some gypsies who had brought him came to take him away."

Jean asked quickly, "Do you know who the men were?"

"No, I do not. Before Gama left, he managed to give me his magic guitar and asked me if I would deliver it to you."

The Danas were intrigued by the story but were still suspicious. Why had Manuel not come to the front door and delivered the instrument? Why had he sneaked into the garden with a skeleton key and bothered to climb the tree to talk to the girls from their second-floor window?

Louise asked him these questions and he said Muja had not wanted him to disturb the household and alert any of his enemies who might be watching the front door.

"Muja said the tribe's fortuneteller had been here and knew your bedroom was near this olive tree."

"Yes, she was here," Jean admitted.

For a moment the Danas wondered how the fortuneteller had learned this. Then they remembered that Jean had set her initialed flight bag on the window sill that morning and forgotten to remove it. The gypsy's keen eyes must have noted this.

Manuel said, "Muja asked me if I thought the guitarist in the band would sell his instrument to him. I guess he hoped to fool the other gypsies. He gave the man a good amount of money and the sale was made."

The musician stopped speaking and waited for the girls to say something. There was silence for several seconds and the man shifted uneasily.

Finally he said, "I would appreciate getting away from here. Would you be willing to keep the magic guitar for Gama? I think he was afraid it would be stolen."

Louise finally spoke up. "I know you'll forgive us for being suspicious. This whole thing seems very strange. Why did you agree to do this?"

Manuel laughed softly. "Believe me I wish I had never promised to do the gypsy's errand for him. I had a hard time getting here and I am sure I was followed. Someone who wants the guitar may be waiting out in the street to do me harm."

Suddenly the Danas felt sorry for the young man. If he were telling the truth, he really had risked great danger in bringing the instrument to the Vasco house.

"Please take it," the young man pleaded. "I cannot stay in this tree forever."

"All right," Louise said. "I believe you are telling the truth, but I should warn you that indeed you are in trouble. Those men who took Gama away are enemies of his. They stole the magic guitar in the first place, then they kidnapped him.

"We think we know who they are, but we are not sure, and besides we cannot find them. Gama is their prisoner. If you ever see them again, report it at once to the police. We're sure they're wanted for robbery and kidnapping."

The accordionist's eyes grew large. With a little cry of fear, he said, "I will do as you say, of course, but I am certainly sorry I ever became involved in this affair. How did two nice girls like you get mixed up with a couple of bandits?"

The Danas did not mention Senhor Sarmento's mystery of the cork thefts, but Louise did tell Manuel of their acquaintanceship on the *Balaska* with Gama Gomes. Jean told the story of all that had happened to him.

The man in the tree gasped. "Poor fellow! I hope he can get away from his captors very soon. They sound like wicked men."

Louise and Jean thought it wise for Manuel to leave now. By letting himself out the garden gate the way he had come in, he might be able to get away without being harmed. Then a thought came to the girls. Had Gama obtained the skeleton key from Torres or Diogo? In any case, it should be left with them.

"Please give us the key," Louise said.

"Certainly," Manuel said. Then suddenly he

"Would you be willing to keep the magic guitar
for Gama?" Manuel asked

gasped. "I forgot to lock the gate. I hope no one followed me in here."

Louise and Jean were fearful. "Where did you leave the magic guitar?"

The accordionist pointed downward. "It's at the foot of the tree."

The girls looked downward and could see the case standing against the trunk.

"I will get it," Manuel said.

He started to climb down. While he was still several feet above the ground, the girls saw an object come sailing through the air. It hit the accordionist hard. He lost his grip on the tree trunk and fell to the ground!

CHAPTER XVII

Unexpected Attack

LOUISE and Jean became fearful when the fallen accordionist did not move. He lay unconscious at the foot of the tree, perhaps fatally injured!

"We must do something fast!" Louise said worriedly.

"Yes," Jean agreed. "But by the time we get all the way downstairs and out into the garden that stone thrower could come in and steal the guitar!"

She said to her sister, "You find something to throw at that man if he comes near the tree. I'll climb down and get the guitar before he can!"

In a moment Jean was out the window and crawling along a branch of the big olive tree. Reaching the trunk, she climbed down quickly.

Meanwhile, Louise had grabbed two sports shoes and now held one in each hand. She wished she could help the injured musician but realized that any intruder should be dealt with to avoid more trouble. The accordionist was groaning, but the sound did not keep the girls from detecting a scraping noise at the gate. It was being opened!

Jean stopped a moment to look at Manuel. "He's alive, anyway!" she thought. "Should I see about getting help to him at once, or shall I grab Gama's precious guitar and hide it?"

She decided to hide the instrument, since she could now hear approaching footsteps. Quick as a flash Jean grabbed up the guitar and fled with it toward a tool house which she had seen in a far corner of the garden.

By this time the intruder was sneaking along among the shadows and had almost reached the tree. From the window above, Louise hurled the sports shoe at him with full force. It hit the man in the back. Puzzled, he stopped and looked around to see who had thrown it.

At the same moment, Louise screamed at the top of her voice to alert the rest of the household. Before the intruder could advance, not only the house but the garden as well was flooded with lights. The man was plainly revealed.

Torres!

He did not hesitate. Realizing that he had been caught red-handed, the gypsy made a beeline for the gate and ran out.

Louise dashed down the stairs. As she reached the bottom step, Senhor Vasco called out from above, "What happened?"

"Look in the garden!" Louise shouted. She herself opened the front door and gazed up and down the street. No one was in sight. Torres had made good his escape!

The Vascos and Sarmentos burst into the garden, amazed to see a groaning figure at the foot of the olive tree.

"Who is he? What happened?" Senhora Vasco asked.

Now that it was safe, Jean had come from the tool house, holding the magic guitar. She explained who Manuel was and why he had come.

"Someone hit him and he fell from the tree."

Louise arrived and told about Torres having entered the garden. "But he fled," she added.

Senhora Vasco suggested that the men carry Manuel into the house. As they carefully picked him up, the musician opened his eyes.

"I am all right," he said in Portuguese.

Nevertheless, he was taken to the living room and laid on a couch. Senhora Vasco suggested getting a doctor.

"I do not need a doctor—really I do not," Manuel said in English, looking toward the Dana girls. "The guitar? Where is it?"

Jean assured the man that it was safe and showed the instrument to him. "I was afraid it would be stolen," he said.

Louise told about her sister having climbed down the tree to retrieve it.

Senhor Sarmento immediately telephoned the police and reported the whole incident and the Danas' suspicions. The officer who answered promised to send two men to the house at once. When they arrived, the officers advised that a burglarproof padlock be put on the gate as soon as possible. They also said that the Ruk tribe of gypsies had not yet been located.

"Then they did not go to Sintra after all," Louise whispered to Jean. She turned to the officers. "We suspect that this man Torres is a member of the Ruk tribe. If you can trace him, he will no doubt lead you to the other members."

The men sighed and one of them said, "When a gypsy decides to disappear, he can certainly make a success of it. He can subsist for a long time through his own wits, without appearing where other people are."

The *policía* asked Manuel if he felt well enough to travel and he declared he did. They said they would follow his car to the musician's home and make sure he was all right. Everyone profusely thanked the accordionist for delivering the guitar. When Senhor Vasco offered to pay him for all his trouble, Manuel smiled and said:

"No, thank you. I am glad to help out a fellow player. Of course I did not expect to risk my life, but everything turned out well. I hope you will come to our restaurant again sometime."

"We surely will," Isabel declared. "But I hope before that time we will have solved the mystery surrounding the magic guitar."

Before going to bed, Senhor Vasco went outside to lock and wire the garden gate. Any intruder would have a hard time getting in and could not do it without attracting the attention of those in the house. Everyone felt more secure now and slept soundly.

In the morning Senhor Sarmento said, "I know you girls feel as if you are marking time until you can locate the gypsy tribe."

The Danas admitted that they did feel stymied and asked if perhaps they could work on the cork mystery.

Isabel's father smiled. "Did you forget this is Sunday? There will be no work today so we cannot investigate the factory or the warehouse except on a weekday."

Senhor Vasco spoke up. "While the girls are here they must do some sightseeing. I think they should make a trip to the quaint fishing village of Nazaré. How about going tomorrow with Senhor Sarmento?" The Danas smiled and accepted the invitation.

Early Monday morning they started out. Senhor Sarmento took the picturesque drive up the coast, going through the resort towns with their beautiful beaches, hotels, and summer homes.

After they had left the village of Estoril, Louise said, "I have a feeling that two men in the black sedan behind us are following on purpose."

"Do you recognize them?" Isabel asked. "I don't."

The Danas shook their heads and Senhor Sarmento said, "I will try them out to prove whether your hunch is right or wrong."

He turned abruptly up a side street and made a detour around a block of the town. The car behind did the same thing.

"Do you have binoculars with you?" Jean asked.

"Yes, I brought a pair," Senhor Sarmento answered. "Isabel, they are in the front compartment."

She opened it and brought out the glasses. Louise, seated in the back, took the glasses and trained them on the pursuers. She thought they looked like gypsies, but neither was Torres or Diogo.

"Perhaps we should forget them," Senhor Sarmento said, trying to calm the girls' fears.

Although the Danas said nothing more, they continued to worry. When they reached the quaint town of Nazaré, they tried to shake off their apprehensive mood.

The girls were intrigued by the fishing village. There was an extremely wide beach, dotted with high-prowed open vessels. Each was gaily painted with various kinds of figures, many of them birds or animals. Moored offshore were several large ships.

Houses were clustered on the hillside above the ocean-front street. There were various types of shops. In some of the doorways sat groups of women. Most of them were dressed in black with black shawls tied over their heads.

"No doubt they are widows of fishermen," Isabel remarked. "They will wear black the rest of their lives—it is the custom."

Suntanned fishermen wearing tasseled stocking caps walked along the street or were busy painting boats.

The Danas and their friends strolled across the beach, where women were busy mending the fishing nets. All wore the traditional seven petticoats. Three little girls who ran up to the visitors coyly lifted a section of their dresses to show the various layers of underskirts.

"Do you speak English?" Louise asked one of them.

"Yes. We learn it in school."

Jean asked, "Have your families from way, way back always lived in Nazaré?"

"For a long time," the second little girl replied. "But centuries ago our people came from Tunisia and sailed all over the world."

Suddenly everyone's attention was directed to a flurry of excitement. Two teams of oxen, standing about twenty feet apart, were being hitched to a long pulley. This was now attached to a gigantic fishing dory which had just arrived and was being dragged up onto the sand.

The third little girl, who had said her name was Bonita, pointed proudly to the crescent-shaped vessel. "My father is captain of that boat." Then, as a thought struck her, she added, "Would you like to go aboard and see all the fish?"

Jean answered at once, "I'd love to." She turned to the others in her group. "How about the rest of you?"

Everyone wanted to go so they hurried forward with their young guide, who waved to her two friends and said, "*Volto mais tarde.*"

Isabel whispered to the Danas, "That means 'See you later!' "

Meanwhile, the child had scooted up a ladder, greeted her father, and presumedly asked his permission to bring her new-found friends aboard. He nodded and one by one the Danas, Isabel, and her father climbed up. Then the little girl climbed down again.

Almost the entire hull of the dory was filled with fish, but the visitors barely had time to ask how big the catch was, when Isabel screamed.

The others turned in her direction just in time to see one of the men who had been following them in the black sedan pick up a large oar. He started to bring it down on the head of Senhor Sarmento.

Louise and Jean jumped forward, grabbed the

man's upraised arms, and held them firmly. He let the oar drop to the deck and it crashed loudly but did not hit anyone.

Isabel excitedly called to the fisherman, "*Pare esse homen!*" Then she broke into English, "Stop that man! Someone get the *polícia!*"

Two strong-armed fishermen leaped forward and held the man. They began to shout angrily at him in Portuguese, but he did not reply.

He glared at Louise and Jean and made kicking motions toward them. Finally he began to mumble in what the Danas assumed was Romany.

Meanwhile, the three little girls had resumed playing near the dory and had heard Isabel's request for help. Bonita cried out, "We get *polícia!*"

The children raced across the sand and returned in a few minutes with two policemen. The actions of the prisoner were quickly related to the officers. They in turn asked him why he had wanted to harm Senhor Sarmento.

The prisoner seemed to show a momentary look of guilt and the Danas hoped he would confess. But they were disappointed. The captor remained silent.

"We will have to search him," one of the policemen spoke up. "He is probably carrying a concealed weapon."

The two fishermen tightened their grip on him as the officers began to empty his pockets. They found several trinkets, a small amount of money, and two colored kerchiefs. One of the policemen produced a long knife from inside the prisoner's shirt.

Louise and Jean gasped. It was a duplicate of the one which had been thrown into the Vascos' front door!

CHAPTER XVIII

Queen Tekla

"THAT knife!" Louise cried out.

The policemen turned to her and one asked, "You recognize it?"

The Danas drew him aside and quickly related the mysterious events which had occurred since their arrival in Lisbon. They were sure, Jean added, that this knife was a duplicate of one which had speared the threatening message to the Vascos' door. Furthermore, they suspected the warning had been sent by a tribe of gypsies called the Ruks.

The officer turned to the seething man. "You a gypsy?" he shouted.

Hatred gleamed in the prisoner's eyes and his lips were set tightly shut. He said nothing. The Danas wondered how he had sneaked aboard without anyone seeing him.

"We will keep this man in our custody until we can get in touch with the Lisbon authorities," one of the policemen said as he handcuffed the prisoner.

When the officers led the man away, the Danas and Sarmentos thanked Bonita and her somewhat confused father for letting them visit the fishing dory. They added their regrets for the mysterious intrusion.

Then Jean suggested to her companions, "Let's see if we can find the man who came with this gypsy."

As soon as the visitors reached the street where their car was parked, they shook the sand from their shoes and began the search. They could find neither the other gypsy nor the black sedan he was driving.

"He was probably watching us," Isabel concluded, "and thought he had better get away quick when the police came."

Senhor Sarmento suggested lunch. He took the girls to a restaurant along the waterfront which specialized in lobster. It was tender and had a most delicious sauce which the Danas were told was a secret of the restaurant.

"I must show you another part of this village," Senhor Sarmento said when they finished eating. "It is called Citio."

He drove them up a steep hill to a promontory from which there was a magnificent view of the harbor. A knot of houses and a church were situated on the attractive site.

"There's an interesting story about the church," Isabel told the Danas as they stepped from the car.

Isabel related how in olden times a knight, Dom Fuas Roupinho, had erected it on the spot where his life had been saved. While on horseback he had been chasing a stag. Although a heavy mist had begun to fall, he kept on. The Dom was determined to get the stag but suddenly his horse stopped short.

"One story says it was the horse's good sense that saved the Dom's life. Another says the Virgin Mary appeared before the animal. In any case, the mist soon lifted and the Dom found himself on the brink of a cliff."

"How scary!" Jean exclaimed.

Senhor Sarmento asked the girls if they would like to go directly home or continue their sightseeing. "Do you think you've had enough excitement for one day?" he inquired, smiling.

The Danas grinned and Louise replied, "It is said, 'Excitement is the spice of life,' and I think I can stand a little more spice today."

"Me too," Jean added. "But perhaps you are tired from so much driving, Senhor Sarmento?"

"On the contrary"—Isabel's father laughed—"I am enjoying myself. Where shall we go next?"

Jean had a ready answer. "Perhaps the Ruk tribe has reached Sintra by now. May we ride on some of the roads in that area? I wish we could find their campsite."

Isabel's father nodded. When they were settled once more in the car he headed in the direction of

Sintra. It was a long ride and they spent over two hours in the town's vicinity. But they saw no gypsies and were about to give up their search when Louise spotted a camp in a grove of trees.

"Please stop, Senhor Sarmento!" she requested.

He pulled up to the side of the road and looked off among the trees, where they could see a camp and people working. There were several small shacks and a fenced-in enclosure containing pigs. To one side tethered horses were grazing. Then, quite unexpectedly, several children appeared and ran toward the visitors' car.

"They are probably going to beg for money," Senhor Sarmento said. "They will put out their hands and wiggle their fingers to indicate that you are to put some coins in their palms."

To everyone's surprise, when the children reached the car they did not raise their hands but merely smiled.

"Do you speak English?" Louise called out.

One little girl shook her head and spoke in Portuguese. Isabel and her father questioned the children.

"Is this the Ruk tribe?"

"No." They pointed to their yellow scarfs, evidently an insigne of this tribe.

Jean had a hunch and said, "Muja."

Instantly the children looked a bit frightened. One asked in English, "You police?"

The Sarmentos assured them they were not.

Louise also had a hunch and decided to try another question. She asked if they knew Tekla.

Hearing this, all the children smiled broadly. Two of them raced off while Isabel talked to the others. Louise confided to Senhor Sarmento, "Gama once told us the name of the queen who gave him his guitar was Tekla."

As she said this, a woman with an air of authority suddenly appeared from among the trees. She wore a long, full black skirt and a gaily colored blouse. A bright-yellow scarf around her head was tied at the nape of her neck. Large earrings dangled to her shoulders, and around her neck were several long chains of gold, silver, and copper beads.

She smiled at the visitors and spoke in halting English, "You know Muja?"

"He also uses the name of Gama Gomes," Louise said.

"Yes."

Many thoughts raced through Louise's mind. Could this be Gama's own tribe, the Kers, and if so, was this Queen Tekla who had given him the magic guitar?

Upon learning that the gypsy woman was really Queen Tekla, the Danas told how they had met the young man. Louise ended by saying, "He loves the magic guitar you gave him and you may be interested to know he has been very successful with it. But I think he is unhappy and lonesome because he never sees you any more."

Sadness crept into the queen's eyes. "I tell you strange story," she said.

Partly in English and partly in Portuguese, she told the visitors that Muja had been banished from the tribe because he did not wish his fellow gypsies to steal again. An old man had befriended him and taught him the right way to live. When the man learned of Muja's banishment, he became friendly with the whole tribe and convinced everyone that Muja had been badly treated.

"We now honest," Queen Tekla said. "No more steal. We want to be friend with Muja."

Jean said enthusiastically, "We hope to see him again. If we do, we will give him your message."

"Where you think you see him?" Tekla asked.

"We think Muja is a prisoner of the Ruk tribe," Louise told her. "We are trying to find him and the police are too."

"Maybe we find Ruk," said Queen Tekla. "They in South sometimes. Clever at stealing and we think they take cork."

The Danas and their friends looked at one another astonished. Was this firsthand proof that the Ruks were the thieves responsible for the shortages in Senhor Sarmento's shipments?

"If you find Muja," Louise spoke up, "tell him that the Danas have a message for him."

The visitors decided not to reveal the fact that the guitar was at the Vascos' house.

"If we find Muja, we have message for him ourselves," the queen said. "We want him to be chief of tribe. Work only honest now."

With wishes of good luck on both sides, the visitors drove off. Before leaving the area, Senhor Sarmento took the girls to the Sintra palace, a strange-looking building of Moorish, Renaissance, and Gothic architecture. Inside, the girls saw the famous magpie room and smiled as they recalled its history.

"Now I must take you to see the room which became the prison for a king," said Senhor Sarmento. "His ambitious brother stole the throne and locked him into one room for the rest of his life."

"Oh, how horrible!" Jean exclaimed.

The girls stood in awe when they reached the upper floor. It was a bleak place, with barred windows and its tiled floor well worn by the imprisoned king who had paced up and down in despair for many years before his death.

"Let's get out of here," said Louise. "This place gives me the willies."

"How about seeing the Peña Castle?" Senhor Sarmento asked.

Louise nodded enthusiastically. "You said it's on top of a mountain. Maybe from there we could spot a gypsy encampment."

He smiled. "And it might just happen to be that of the Ruks."

He and the girls went out to the car. Jean suggested that before leaving, they ask some of the shopkeepers in the town if any gypsies had been there.

"That is a good idea," he agreed.

The Danas hurried across the street and questioned not only the shopkeepers but also pedestrians. In each case the answer was No. Disappointed, the girls went back to the car.

"No luck," Jean reported.

In a short time Senhor Sarmento turned from the main road and started climbing the steep wooded hill that led to Peña Castle. Camellias bloomed in profusion in water gardens along the way.

"What a beautiful approach!" Louise murmured.

Senhor Sarmento parked the car near the top, saying they would have to walk the rest of the way up the cobblestoned driveway. A guard let them enter through the drawbridge and they climbed still higher to reach the wide piazza and stare in amazement at the Arab minarets, Renaissance cupolas, and Gothic towers of the castle.

"Look at the dragon figures!" Isabel exclaimed, gazing at the tremendously high wall of the castle with the fantastic carvings.

Louise began to snap pictures, while Jean walked out into one of the sentry boxes and looked down at the surrounding countryside. Although she could see for miles and miles, her keen eyes failed to detect any spot where gypsies were living.

After a hurried trip inside the castle to see the old king's and queen's rooms, Senhor Sarmento glanced at his watch. "We must return home," he said, "or we will be late to dinner."

"It's been an exciting day," Louise remarked. "And we did pick up a wonderful clue. Now if we can only find Muja."

The next morning Isabel's father said he was going down to his warehouse at the dock.

"Would you girls like to go along?" he asked. "Perhaps you could pick up a clue to the thieves."

His daughter and the Danas eagerly accepted.

"Would it be all right if I brought my camera along?" Louise asked. "I'd like to take a few pictures of the factory."

Senhor Sarmento gave his permission heartily. When they reached the dock, a freighter was being loaded with cork products from the warehouse.

Presently the girls noticed that Senhor Sarmento was checking an invoice with a workman. The original order was short several bales.

As the argument became heated, Louise said to the other girls, "Let's go into the warehouse and look around." She grinned. "We might even find the thief!"

They roamed around inside the building, where bales and cartons containing various cork products were piled high.

Suddenly Isabel called to the Danas, "Come!

Look here!" She motioned to several ripped bales. The contents were gone.

"The thief has been here!" Louise exclaimed. "We must report this to your father immediately!"

The girls hurried off, but they had not gone far when Jean grabbed Louise's arm and pointed.

Behind a high stack a man with a long knife was slashing open a bale!

CHAPTER XIX

Double Take

THE girls sped toward the man on tiptoe. He had finished ripping open the bale and now began to scoop the contents into a large kerchief which lay on the floor.

"Stop that!" Louise cried out.

The man looked up. Realizing he had been caught, he held the knife menacingly but said nothing. The girls had never seen him before, but there was the tattoo of a tree on his forehead.

"He's a Ruk!" Jean whispered.

The girls did not dare advance any farther, so they began to shout, "Help! Help!"

Their cries sent the man running, but it also brought dockworkers scurrying into the warehouse. The gypsy, cornered, tried to fend off his captors by waving the knife in front of them.

A workman sneaked up behind the thief and

overpowered him. Everyone sighed in relief as his weapon was taken away.

"What was he doing?" another man asked.

Louise pointed first to the empty bale and then to the gypsy's makeshift sack. By this time Senhor Sarmento had rushed up. When he heard the girls had spotted the thief, he was loud in his praise.

"We will call the police," he added.

Jean whispered to him, "If we let this man go, could he be trailed? He might lead us to the Ruk tribe."

The manufacturer smiled and patted Jean on the shoulder. "Ordinarily your idea would be a good one, but gypsies can disappear like magic. You remember what the police officer said at the Vascos'. This man probably would not return home until it was dark. He would use every shortcut he knew. It would be impossible to follow him."

The harbor police were called and immediately took the gypsy into custody. Like the one captured at Nazaré, he too refused to talk.

Louise turned to Senhor Sarmento. "If the gypsies are stealing the cork, what are they doing with it? Surely they could not use so much of it themselves."

"You're right, Louise. I have been working on a theory. The gypsies may be selling it to some unscrupulous dealer. I've told this to the detective working on our case and he'll check it out."

"Are the profits large enough to make the thefts worthwhile?" Jean put in.

"Not large, but frequent," Senhor Sarmento answered.

The Danas decided to continue their hunt for clues in the warehouse. Louise snapped flashbulb pictures of the factory's floor plan and close-ups of the area where the torn bales lay.

It was evident that more than one thief had been there because one man could not have handled such a large quantity of cork products.

"Guess that's about it," Louise said, moving the knob to be ready for the final snapshot. But suddenly her finger slipped and the shutter clicked.

"Oh no!" Louise said. Her eyes were still blinking from the light of the flashbulb when Jean asked what had happened. "I just ruined my last picture."

In the meantime Isabel had gone off a short distance from them and was making a search of her own. She cried out excitedly and the Danas rushed to her side.

"Now what is it?" Jean asked.

"Look on the wall!"

Two symbols had been chalked on!

"The first one means men travelers," Louise said quickly. "I wonder what the other one means."

Isabel copied the symbols on a piece of paper, and the three girls hurried off to find Senhor Sarmento. When they told him of their discovery, he suggested they take a taxi to the Vascos' home and check in the gypsy book.

"I must stay here a while longer," he explained.

Isabel led the Danas outside and hailed a taxi. On the way, Louise left her roll of film at a camera store not far from the Vascos' house. The clerk promised to have the pictures developed by that afternoon. As soon as the three girls reached home, they hurried in to find the now-familiar gypsy reference book.

"The second symbol on the warehouse wall stands for well or fountain," Isabel pointed out.

The three friends discussed the various possibilities of the symbols' meaning.

"My first guess," said Jean, "is that this is a message one or more gypsies left for the rest of their tribe."

"I agree," Louise added. "The Ruks are moving and can be found at some particular place where there's water or a well or fountain. Isabel, do you know of a likely one offhand that would be a good meeting place?"

"Not at this moment," she answered. "But remember Gama Gomes's note said the tribe was moving to Sintra. There could be such a spot somewhere in that vicinity."

The trio went to consult Senhora Vasco. At

once she had a suggestion. "It might be the huge kitchen in the monastery at Alcobaça, with a stream running through. It's just outside of Sintra. Or it could be the great fountain in the Batalha monastery."

"Could the gypsies hide out in either place?" Jean asked.

"Possibly. Both are enormous and not used any more. There are a few tourists at this time of year, but most likely no one would be around."

The Danas were eager to set off at once. But Isabel's aunt insisted they wait for Senhor Sarmento to return.

"I would not want you to go anywhere without a man," she said. "Too many things have happened to make it safe for you girls to travel alone. Besides, it's almost lunchtime."

Louise and Jean were easily persuaded by her last comment. They were very hungry! As they were about to enjoy a cheese omelet prepared especially for the American visitors, Senhor Sarmento came in to join them. After hearing the story, he was as eager as the girls to make the trip to Alcobaça and Batalha.

"There's a very interesting story about Alcobaça," he said.

"In the naves to the left and right just below the altar are the tombs of two of the world's greatest lovers. According to the story, Prince Pedro was in love with a beautiful woman named Inès. Be-

cause she was Spanish, his father would not allow
him to marry her. Later, Pedro became king. The
courtiers were afraid Inès and her brothers were
planning to double-cross the Portuguese, so they
murdered her."

The girls groaned. "How dreadful!" Jean said
quickly. "I'm sure the king was heartbroken."

"Indeed he was," Senhor Sarmento replied. "He
had Inès crowned queen after her death, and made
all the courtiers kiss her hand. Then he ordered
that when he died, his body was to be buried so
that his feet would be exactly opposite those of his
beloved Inès."

"What was the purpose of that?" Louise asked.

"King Pedro said that on the day of resurrec-
tion, when the two of them arose, they would be
facing each other."

"That's a romantic love story indeed, but certainly a tragic one," Louise commented.

"I guess we should leave now," Senhor Sarmento said as he rose from the table.

Louise asked, "May I phone the camera shop?
The clerk promised he would have my film developed by this afternoon."

Senhor Sarmento admitted he was curious to see
the snapshots and joked about starting a picture
scrapbook of his warehouse. Louise went off to
telephone the shop and returned smiling.

"The pictures are ready. We'll be able to look at
them on the way to Alcobaça."

"I am amazed the shop was able to comply with your request so quickly," Senhora Vasco said.

Jean giggled. "It's the way Sis bats her eyelashes."

Everyone laughed at the comment. Then, waving good-by to Senhora Vasco, the Danas and Sarmentos drove off in the Vascos' rented car.

They stopped at the camera shop to pick up the developed film, then began the drive to the monastery. Louise slid her pictures out of their envelope and sifted through them. She studied the several ways of entering and leaving the warehouse, then passed the snapshots to Jean.

"Senhor Sarmento," she asked, "do you have a night watchman in the warehouse?"

"No, we do not. I suppose that is very foolish of us. But we do keep the factory well locked at night. And none of the locks have been broken."

"Um-hum."

"Why? Are you suggesting that the thieves have skeleton keys they use at night?" Senhor Sarmento queried.

"Not exactly," Louise replied. "I have an idea—"

"Wait a minute," Jean interrupted her sister. "Look at this!" She held out a blurred picture.

Louise glanced at it quickly. "That must be the one I ruined."

Jean urged, "Take a close look. Don't you see the man's face peering from behind that pile of cartons in the far corner? Seems a bit suspicious to me."

"What's this?" Senhor Sarmento asked, leaning his head back slightly to hear the girls' conversation better.

By now Louise was studying the photograph intently. The man's face was not clear and she suggested the picture be enlarged after they returned home.

"Here. I just happen to have this with me," Isabel's father said as he held up a small magnifying glass he had taken from his pocket. He chuckled. "I guess I'm getting the hang of this detective work!"

The girls laughed and Louise trained the glass over the picture. She gasped in amazement. "It's Diogo!"

"What!" cried Isabel.

As she and Jean took turns identifying the face in the snapshot, Senhor Sarmento exclaimed, "This practically solves the mystery!"

"It's a big help," Jean agreed.

Presently Louise said, "There must be a lot of men in the theft ring. To take so much cork so frequently the Ruks must be stealing day and night. Perhaps they use lookouts and it must have been Diogo this time. He probably stays in the factory at closing time and lets his fellow thieves in at night."

"And helps them carry out the bales of stolen

cork products as well," Senhor Sarmento added. "A real possibility, Louise. And now let's hope we find the Ruks."

After a long drive he pulled up in front of the ancient monastery of Alcobaça. The Danas were amazed at its size.

"Nine hundred and ninety-nine monks once lived here," Isabel's father said.

"Why not a thousand?" Jean asked.

Senhor Sarmento smiled. "When they had a meeting of all the monks, the bishop made the thousandth. By the way, they were allowed to talk only one hour a day."

"How awful!" said Jean.

The four visitors went inside. At once a guide appeared and offered to show them around.

"Have any gypsies been here?" Jean asked him.

"No. They never come to a place like this."

He led them down the 344-foot-long nave with its 65-foot-high ceiling to the marble sarcophagi of Queen Inès and King Pedro.

"Isn't she beautiful?" Isabel whispered, gazing at the statue of the lovely sleeping figure lying at the top, a crown on her head.

"And he's so handsome," Louise murmured.

The guide moved off and they followed him through a side door to a courtyard garden with cloisters on each side. Enormous rooms opened off one. It was the kitchen that held them spellbound.

"It's tremendous!" Louise said in awe.

An extremely long spit had been built in the center of the room. From it rose a chimney which extended through the roof at least three stories above.

"Six oxen can be roasted at once on this spit," the guide told them.

The Danas grinned and Louise commented, "Those monks certainly lived well."

"Yes, they did," he agreed.

At the far end of the long room there was a fairly deep catch basin into which water drained from the river. Senhor Sarmento said this was one of the spots his sister-in-law thought the gypsy symbols might refer to.

"Ugh!" Isabel exclaimed as something slithered into the basin. "What's that? It looks like a huge snake!"

"It's an eel," her father replied. "Long ago this was one source of food for the monks."

The Danas saw nothing to indicate a clue to the Ruks.

After visiting other rooms and finding no evidence that gypsies were hiding in the monastery, the Danas and their friends set off for Batalha not many miles away. This vacant monastery, built over thirteen hundred years ago, stood on open ground, its gold-colored walls gleaming starkly in the sunlight.

As soon as they entered the great building with its many stained-glass windows, a man in uniform stalked up to them and announced he would be their guide.

"Very good," said Senhor Sarmento. "My daughter and I have been through here before and we'll be glad to rest in the garden while our friends go with you."

They all followed the young guide through the sanctuary and out to the cloistered garden which was laid out in geometrical designs with green hedges. Louise and Jean went on. They paused for a moment to pay their respects in an inner room to the grave of Portugal's Unknown Soldier, guarded day and night by two live soldiers.

At the end of the cloister, Jean grabbed Louise's arm. "The fountain!" she whispered.

Water splashed down over the enormous three-tiered bronze piece.

Jean said to the guide, "Have you seen any gypsies around here?"

"No, I have not."

"Do you know of a gypsy tribe called the Ruks who might be living in the vicinity?"

"No, but there is a man here who can tell you. I will take you to him."

The sisters, thrilled that they might at last locate the mysterious tribe, followed the guide through another door into a garden, across to another building, up a stairway, and along a corridor. Presently he came to a heavy wooden door and opened it.

"Just go right in there," he said.

The place was dimly lighted and before the girls could accustom their eyes to the darkness, they heard the great door close behind them and a key turn in the lock.

Jean and Louise ran to the entrance and pounded on the heavy door. "Let us out of here!"

The man laughed. They tried the knob, but it was no use. They were prisoners!

"Who are you?" Jean called.

There was no answer.

"You're not a guide!" Louise added firmly.

"Neither the real guide nor your gypsy friend can help you now," came the gruff reply.

The girls listened in despair as their captor's footsteps faded down the corridor.

CHAPTER XX

The Guitar's Secret

PANICKING, Louise and Jean pounded on the door and kept screaming, "Help! Let us out!"

But their cries were in vain. Even if someone heard them, how could he help them? The heavy door was locked. They thought of the regular guide, who had no doubt been imprisoned. How far away was he?

Finally the girls ceased pounding and crying out and calmed down. "We'll have to think up something," Jean said. She added hopefully, "When Senhor Sarmento and Isabel miss us, they'll begin to look around."

Louise was not so optimistic. "I wouldn't count on their finding us," she said. She began to study the room for some means of escape. Finally her eyes focused on a small window high in the side wall.

Jean, guessing what her sister was thinking, remarked, "No chance of getting out that way."

"No," Louise agreed, "but how about our writing a note and throwing it out the window?"

"Goodness knows where it will land," Jean said, but conceded that it was their only chance. If the note fell into the hands of their enemies, they could be no worse off than they were now.

Louise took a notebook from her purse, wrote a short message on one of the sheets, and tore it out. She folded it, then handed the paper to her sister. "Jean, suppose you stand on my shoulders and toss this note out the window."

Louise crouched so that Jean could swing onto her sister's shoulders. Louise then raised up. Jean gripped hold of a bar with one hand, and with her other hand, threw the note away from the building. She watched the paper flutter out of sight, then climbed down.

The two girls seated themselves on the floor and waited hopefully. Presently Jean said, "It's just possible that Gama Gomes is a prisoner here too."

As if in answer to Jean's remark, she and Louise heard muffled cries for help. Were they from Gama Gomes or the imprisoned guide or someone else?

Meanwhile, the Sarmentos had been waiting in the patio garden and were growing impatient. They thought it was time for the Danas to return. Just then they saw the girls' guide coming in their direction without Jean or Louise. Isabel and her father hurried up to him.

"Where are our friends?" Isabel asked.

The man answered nonchalantly, "They wanted to look around some more and said they would meet you at the car." He walked off and disappeared.

In a few minutes the Sarmentos returned to their car. They waited and waited for the Danas.

"What can be keeping them?" Isabel's father asked.

"I'm getting worried," Isabel said finally. "I think we should go back inside and look for them."

They stepped out of the car and walked toward the entrance of the monastery. Reaching it, they found the great door locked.

"Oh dear!" Isabel exclaimed. "Louise and Jean are in there! We must get them out!"

Senhor Sarmento was alarmed also. He had a strong feeling that something had gone amiss. "We must go to the village police to report this incident at once," he said.

A few minutes later they saw a number of gypsy men coming their way. They were wearing yellow scarfs. As they drew near, Isabel cried out, "They're Kers from Queen Tekla's tribe!"

Senhor Sarmento stopped the car and spoke to the gypsies.

"We have just had a fight with the Ruk tribe,"

their leader said. "We have learned from them that Muja is a prisoner in Batalha."

"What!" Isabel exclaimed. Turning to her father, she added fearfully, "Maybe that's what happened to Louise and Jean!"

Senhor Sarmento turned around and went back to the monastery with the gypsies. But try as they might, they could not get inside. While they were discussing what to do, a man came around the corner of the building, holding a piece of paper.

"I found this on the ground," he said, coming up to the Sarmentos. "It is in English and I cannot read it."

"It's from Louise and Jean!" Isabel exclaimed. "They *are* prisoners in the monastery!"

She asked the man who had brought the note if he knew how they could get inside the building. He told them that there was an elderly man in the village who had a key to the great door.

"I will be glad to help," he said. "I will ride with you to the village and introduce you to the man."

It was not long before they reached his house and explained the problem. He was surprised to learn the monastery was locked, but went for his keys and came to the car. Senhor Sarmento decided that they should have some policemen with them and went to headquarters to make his request.

The whole group hurried to the monastery. The door was opened and everyone raced inside. The man who had found the note knew how to reach the section from which the note had been thrown and led the way.

"Help is here! Where are you?" he cried out.

To the joy and amazement of the searchers, four voices answered. Two of them belonged to the Dana girls, one to Muja, and the fourth to the imprisoned guide. All were quickly freed.

At first the gypsy minstrel shied away from members of his tribe, but when he was told of their conversion to an honest life, he was overjoyed.

The Danas stood by smiling as they watched the greetings of affection among the gypsy men. Finally Muja came to the girls and thanked them profusely for solving the mystery.

"But I will never be happy until I have my magic guitar again," he said.

The two young detectives grinned and Louise said, "We have a nice surprise for you. Your guitar is safe at the Vascos' home."

The minstrel sighed with relief. He said he had not been able to contact the accordionist since asking him to deliver the instrument to the Danas. Torres had lied to Muja and told him that he had stolen it from the garden.

"He is such a wicked man," Louise said. "Have the police taken all the Ruks into custody, including Torres and Diogo?"

Muja put the question to his fellow gypsies. His face was creased by a broad grin as he said, "All the men were taken to jail by the *policia do trans-ito*—our Federal police."

"Ask your friends," Jean said, "if the Ruks confessed that they had been stealing Senhor Sarmento's cork products."

A lengthy conversation in Romany followed. Finally the Danas and Sarmentos got the full story. An unscrupulous dealer on the outskirts of Lisbon was buying the cork products and raw cork at a fraction of their real value. He was putting them into his own boxes and shipping them to the United States.

Since Torres and Diogo were experts in making skeleton keys, it had been easy for the Ruks to enter Senhor Sarmento's warehouse, especially at night. Undisturbed, they had carefully opened the bales and cartons, taken out the cork products, substituted wadded newspaper, and fastened the containers again.

"And no one detected this until the cork products were unpacked in New York," Louise remarked.

"That's right," said Senhor Sarmento. "The clerk Roberto, who checked outgoing cargo from Lisbon, declared the thefts were not done here. The prisoners say he was also a Ruk in cahoots with them. During the past few days the thieves in desperation became bolder and careless. That led to their capture."

The Danas were told that Fero and Yerko were

members of the tribe. Fero had poisoned the donkey to scare Sarmento and the girls from continuing their detective work.

Jean asked, "Why did Torres attack you, Senhor Sarmento?"

He asked the Ker gypsies, who told him Torres had hoped to injure him so severely he would not be able to do any detective work. "By this time Torres had also made up his mind to get the magic guitar and wanted no interference."

"Who sent the radiogram to you on the *Balaska*, telling about two thieves being on board?" Jean queried.

"The clerk Roberto. It seems Diogo tried to discredit him with the tribe. Angry, Roberto sent the message for spite."

Louise looked at Muja. "How did you obtain a skeleton key to the Vascos' gate?"

The minstrel laughed. "Torres was bragging about the key one day so I helped myself to it!"

"Father," said Isabel, "this capture of the Ruks is marvelous news. Now you have nothing more to worry about."

"How true!" Senhor Sarmento said. "And I have you Danas to thank for everything."

Louise and Jean smiled modestly and changed the subject. They asked Muja whether Torres and Diogo had admitted being responsible for the various vicious events on shipboard for which the Danas had suspected them. Muja nodded. Diogo had released Torres from the brig. Then, by radio-gram prearrangement, he had escaped with the guitar in a fellow worker's stolen boat, the *Rio Rosa*, just before the *Balaska* docked. Torres had bribed the pastry cook and had entered Captain Dana's quarters. The two gypsies had also stolen money from Gama Gomes in New York and left gypsy symbols on the ship and in the warehouse.

They confessed to everything they had been accused of doing.

The two men carried rubber masks and wigs with them. Using the Portuguese names of Torres and Diogo, they had been sent to the United States to check on Senhor Sarmento and steal from his warehouse there. They had panicked upon learning he was going to Portugal to investigate the cork thefts.

"Torres and Diogo knew about me," Muja went on, "and planned to rob me and steal my magic guitar. It was a coincidence that we all came over here on the same ship."

As the group were leaving, Jean declared that this was the most exciting day in her life.

"You mean so far," said Louise, feeling sure that another baffling mystery would soon come their way. It did and was called *The Phantom Surfer*.

The following day an invitation came from Queen Tekla for the Danas, the Sarmentos, and the Vascos to attend a celebration at the gypsy camp and bring Muja's guitar.

"Maybe," said Jean, as they were driving out to the camp, "we'll find out how Queen Tekla made the guitar a magic instrument."

There was a great and delicious feast with much singing and guitar playing. Finally the queen said, "I think now you all deserve to know the secret of the minstrel's guitar."

The handsome woman smiled as she explained the secret which had been handed down from mother to daughter for several generations. She had deftly strung a second set of strings beneath those on the top of the guitar. They were hidden and had gone unnoticed. The ends were fastened to the same tuning pegs, so that the two sets were kept in perfect unison. When the instrument was played, the second set of strings gave a haunting, overtone quality to the music.

"It's beautiful," Louise said. "Why don't you patent your idea, make special guitars, and sell them? I am sure they would bring a good income to your tribe."

"Yes, a fine idea. I will try that," Queen Tekla replied.

The festivities ended with a surprise for Louise and Jean. Muja had composed a beautiful ballad in their honor. When he played and sang it, the two girls had difficulty holding back tears of joy.

"That is very beautiful," Louise said when he finished. "Please, may I have a copy of it."

The gypsy promised to mail them one. He also

promised that when he came back to the United States on a tour, to include Oak Falls, where the Danas lived.

"And please," Jean spoke up, "if we're away at school, will you give a concert at Starhurst?"

"I certainly will," the minstrel promised.

As the gathering was about to disperse, Queen Tekla stood up and held her hand in the air for silence.

"Before I say good night," her musical voice intoned, "I want to announce another great celebration. Tomorrow we shall make Muja chief of the Ker tribe!"